GRIM AND BARE IT

THE ACCIDENTAL REAPER MYSTERY SERIES, BOOK 1

MISTY EVANS

Grim and Bare It, The Accidental Reaper Mystery Series, Book 1

Misty Evans

©2022

ISBN: 978-1-948686-52-5

Print ISBN: 978-1-948686-53-2

Cover Art by EDH Graphics & Fanderclai Design

Formatting by Beach Path Publishing, LLC

Editing by Elizabeth Neal, Patricia Essex

ONE

Rain fell softly, patting against the windowpanes of the classroom. Professor O'Leary's voice was a deep resonance accompanying the lullaby. My eyelids kept drooping, the ancient heater of the college's annex warming the cool fall night to the point of baking us all.

"Chloe?" Nita's urgent whisper sounded distant. The jab of her pen was not, catching me in the ribs. "Wake up!"

I snapped to, discovering O'Leary and half my fellow Advanced Animal Anatomy students staring at me. Two of the girls at the table in front of ours snickered and rolled their eyes. By the deep crease between the Professor's brows, it seemed dozing was frowned upon.

Sitting up from the slouch I'd fallen into, I surreptitiously checked the corner of my mouth for drool, finding a bit that I wiped away. I grabbed the end of my braid, hanging over my shoulder and rubbed it between my finger and thumb—and old habit when I was anxious.

Since O'Leary's gaze implied he was waiting for something, I assumed he'd asked a question. "Sorry." I cleared my throat. The whiteboard held a simplistic drawing of a canine leg with a circle around a crudely disfigured knee joint. "The patella is out of place, as is often found in small breeds due to genetics, and commonly requires surgery to correct." I described the easily and frequently performed operation in brief detail, finishing with, "Recovery takes two to four weeks and low impact exercises are recommended as therapy."

Somewhere in all of that, I must have answered whatever question he'd posed. "Very good," he replied. His forehead stayed furrowed, but his eyes left me and roamed the space. He continued on with his baritone voice as he put others on the spot.

While my hometown of approximately twenty-thousand people boasted an historical downtown, haunted ghost tours of the dozen archaic cemeteries, and had one of Louisiana's best veterinary schools, locals of Dante's Grove were often referred to as Hell's Rejects by outsiders. Observing several of my fellow students pretending to take notes on their school-issued laptops while actually viewing videos of others being pranked around campus made me consider that the nickname wasn't far off the mark. To add to the not-quite-New Orleans-yet-still-creepy vibe we had going, there was currently a supposed serial killer on the loose in our sleepy town. The mayor and Chamber of Commerce, along with the police, were throwing everything they had into not losing the sliver of tourism that kept many businesses alive.

After O'Leary closed out the lecture, I yawned and hefted my backpack onto a shoulder while texting for a ride. Nita threw an arm around me as we moseyed down the nearly empty corridor to the stairs. Her purple dyed hair was in a knot at the back of her head, and her honey brown eyes studied me with every glance she snuck my way. A threesome of our classmates laughed and talked ahead of us, and the overhead fluorescent light flickered and hummed, as if threatening us to hurry or it would plunge us into darkness.

"Still not sleeping?" she asked.

Nita and I were a few years older than most of the others. She'd originally started in pre-med, decided she liked animals more than humans, and switched her major. For me, I had to save money, working at my parent's veterinary clinic for several years, before I could afford classes. My dad was always adamant I not take out loans.

Tugging the front of my jacket tighter as a gust of chilly, damp air rushed down the stairs from the threesome's exit, I sighed. "A few hours here and there."

"You can't keep this up." She gently plucked at one of my locks that had escaped my braid. She was always totally put together, even on nights like this, while on my best days I was a mess. "You have to sleep, Morticia," she teased. Her obsession with the Addams Family was only one of the reasons we'd been friends since kindergarten. "Chronic sleep deprivation can lead to heart arrhythmias, mental confusion, high blood pressure, a weakened immune system, and low sex drive."

With the last pronouncement, she elbowed me in the ribs and winked.

I didn't even have a spot in my calendar to look at boys, much less hook up with one. "Thank you, Gomez, or should I say, Dr. WebMD? My immunity system and love life are perfectly fine."

"So you accepted Todd's invite to the Halloween party?"

"Do I look that desperate?"

The sigh that left her lips echoed in the stairwell. "You

are that desperate. You work two jobs, on top of volunteering for Helping Paws and attending classes. It's no wonder you can't sleep. Did you try the tea and supplements my guru recommended?"

"Yes," I fudged. I couldn't even remember where I'd put the stash he'd pushed off on me at our latest visit to his metaphysical shop, but I *had* sniffed it before losing it. That totally counted, right? "I think they're helping already."

The sharpness in her eyes said she didn't believe me.

"Once I'm finished with school, I'll get a real, adult, full-time job with benefits—vacation, health insurance, the whole package." I hated that I felt the need to wipe awaythe worry on her face, but I did. "I'll stop living on minimum wage and free coffee. I promise to make you proud."

She glanced out the glass doors, the rain a deluge now. Her pert nose screwed up and she visibly shivered. "Speaking of fuel, want to hit the shop for a nightcap?"

We both worked at The Smoking Bean, and the quaint coffee shop had become our home away from home. We spent many late nights there studying, and used it for early morning sanity runs before tests. "You're harassing me about sleep, but you want to pump me full of caffeine?"

Her lips firmed with chastisement. "I'll make you a Baby Bomb, warm, soothing, and decaf. The spices will induce peaceful slumber."

The specialty drink she'd come up with was a hit with the New Age crowd who loved the spiced Chai mixture swimming in their choice of soy, almond, or oat milk. She recruited more and more fans at her yoga studio and her guru's store by always taking one with her to tease them. I checked the time—we'd be back there in nine hours per our schedules. "Tempting, but I'll take a raincheck—no pun intended." I cocked my chin at the downpour.

She lifted the hood of her deep rose jacket that looked amazing against her tan skin. "That was well below your normal snark quality line. You really do need sleep. Please tell me you didn't pick up an extra shift at the bone house."

"At least the dead don't harass me, unlike some of the living I know." The morgue was quiet most nights, and Uncle Morty, a pathologist who worked for the only hospital in the fifty mile radius, paid me well and brought me food from my aunt every weekend. The only requirement of my position was answering the phone and handling light paperwork. Which hadn't been so light with the rash of bodies the Grim Reaper—as our serial killer had been named by the media—had produced in the past month. The night shifts didn't interfere with my classes or The Bean's hours, and I normally had plenty of downtime to study and complete homework there. "No work tonight." I crossed my fingers, hoping it stayed that way. "Just a date with a warm bath and a good book. Then nighty-night."

Nita hugged me, suffocating me in the scent of her citrus perfume. "I worry about you, Morticia." Lightning flashed and she released her too-tight grip. "Come on, I'll take you home."

Able to breathe again, I checked my phone. "My ride is almost here. I'll see you in the morning."

"You sure?"

"Ms. Frost?" Professor O'Leary buttoned his puffy coat and adjusted his briefcase as he ascended the steps behind us. "Do you have a moment?"

Uh oh. I instinctively sensed this wouldn't be good.

Nita arched a dark brow in question, but I waved her off. "Go on. I'll be fine."

"Text me when you get home." Acting like my mother

was normal for her, and she hugged me again before reluctantly braving the storm.

Turning away from the wind and rain her exit provided, I faced our teacher. My fingers gravitated to my braid again and I forced them away. "What's up, Professor?"

Dr. Jamison O'Leary was a former veterinarian who'd decided the world of academia was more his speed. I wasn't sure why, but he'd switched professions and insisted no one call him 'doctor.'

He smoothed a hand over his thick salt and pepper hair and glanced at my shoes before he cleared his throat. "I know how important finishing your degree is for you, especially under the constraints you've faced." His tone suggested a *but* was next. "However,"—*yep, there it is*—"your grades this semester are slipping. Your normally in-depth papers are, well, honestly, Chloe, they're fluff pieces, and you continually doze off in class."

Embarrassed, I peeked at the water-slicked parking lot. He was uncomfortable delivering his speech, but it was accurate. *Where is that ride?* "It's been a rough year."

He looked at me over the top of his reading glasses, still on the end of his nose. His pale blue eyes were full of concern...and pity. "I'm aware of your situation, and I commend you for not dropping out entirely. Your parents would be proud of you." The second *but* was about to fall. "Nevertheless, perhaps you've been pushing yourself too hard."

Next, he'd trade places with the counselor I saw once a month. My aunt and uncle had insisted on it, after I'd stopped talking when my parents died. Eighteen months later, I still had bi-weekly meetings with her. Dr. Maxwell had recently suggested I was avoiding my feelings by keeping myself so busy I didn't have time to deal with grief. She wasn't wrong.

At least I was able to speak again. It had been touch and go for a while. Just thinking about it made me anxious. I twirled the end of my braid. "I have a plan, sir, a timeline. Your concern is appreciated, but I assure you, I can handle whatever comes my way. Nothing is more important to me right now than reopening my parents' clinic. My dad faced impossible odds when he started Frosty Paws Small Animal Clinic, and I'm just as determined"—*and maybe as bull-headed*—"as he was."

Lightning flashed behind us, illuminating the campus. My ride was still AWOL, but the cardboard dryness in my mouth this conversation had produced made my tongue thick. Raising my hood, I pushed the metal bar to open the door. "Good night, Professor."

His response, if he gave one, was drowned out by a clap of thunder.

TWO

In my small, nondescript apartment a little while later, I sank into gallons of warm water, inhaling lavender from the bath salts I'd added. A candle burned on the corner of the tiny tub, the flames sending a flickering shadow over the 1960s pink tiles.

My muscles melted and I slid farther into the depths, heaving a tired sigh. I'd actually found Nita's offering from her guru, and made a cup of tea with it. Smelled terrible and I'd had to add a dash of honey, but I'd held my nose and downed it, along with two of the dubious supplements. Odds that the concoction would send me to dreamland were slim, but at least I wouldn't feel guilty about lying to her.

O'Leary's words echoed in my mind, the memory of my parents' car crash pinching my heart. It was always "their" crash, even though I'd also been in the vehicle when it tumbled over the side of the road. We'd hit the metal siderail like a wrecking ball, taking out the barrier that should have stopped us, before pencil-rolling down the steep incline. I'd walked away with a concussion, nothing more. My parents had both died. Life wasn't fair, but saying those words didn't change anything.

Submerging my head so all I heard was the soft vacuum of the water, I shifted out of pity mode and back to neutral. This was my go to, the only way I'd found to keep the awful memories at bay and force myself to move forward. *Bath—calm—sleep.* No agenda, no obligations, no worries. I just needed to blank out on the whole thinking/feeling front. Maybe tonight I'd finally sleep and the knot in my chest would loosen a fraction.

My lids grew heavy and I came up enough to breathe again. Limbs loose, the muscles softened around my bones as I kept my mind empty.

Floating in warm oblivion, my left brain tried to keep pulling me back to the past. I told it to let me rest for a few moments, willing myself, the bath, the tea, all of it, to make me feel normal again.

The fragile peace lasted all of five seconds. A loud bang and a piercing call, both slightly muffled by the bath, made my eyes fly open. "Chloe! Where are you?"

I shot up, sending water lapping over the sides, as I heard Vera, my downstairs landlady, approaching with heavy steps.

My apartment had two entrances—one that led directly outside to a flight of wooden stairs and a second interior staircase inside her two-story home. While I'd locked both doors, she had a key and absolutely no qualms about letting herself in. She'd once been a floor monitor in an all-girls school and hovered somewhere between treating me like a younger sister and a wayward child in need of mothering. I got that a lot now that my own mom was no longer here.

Her meaty fist banged on the door, making me jump,

although I'd anticipated it. "Miss Pickles ran off! I can't find her anywhere. You have to help, Chloe!"

Wrapping a towel around my dripping torso, I reined in my frustration. Her cat went for regular jaunts around the neighborhood, and this was the third time this month she'd escaped. She'd been spayed, yet I suspected she had a boy toy or two in the area. "Even the feline is seeing more action than I am," I muttered to myself.

"What?" Another double rap on the door. "Chloe? Did you hear me?"

Half the country could. "I'll be out in a minute."

"Please hurry. She hates the rain!"

Yet, she left the nice, dry house to go out in it. In record time, I jerked on a pair of joggers and gave the now cooling bath water a forlorn glance before pulling the plug.

Vera paced in my kitchen, the room no larger than a sardine can and her generous size making it impossible for me to squeeze in. "Hand me the tuna pouch from the upper left cabinet," I instructed.

Face splotchy from crying, she obliged, screwing up her nose at the bare shelves. "When was the last time you bought groceries?"

Snagging the item, I ignored the question. "Where did you see her headed?"

She wobbled behind me, following me to the exit door. "Her usual spot—the playground."

Hastily, I re-braided my hair and slipped on a rain poncho before grabbing my small flashlight and taser. I rummaged in my desk drawer until I found my headlamp and stuck that in my other pocket. Miss Pickles was fast and nimble for her ten years and I'd need both hands available to catch her.

The air temperature had dropped significantly, but the

rain had slowed to a mist. The lights of the park three blocks away glowed cheerily through the gloom.

Vera stood on the stoop as I headed that direction. "Be careful," she called. "That reaper murderer is still on the loose!"

My stomach growled and I wished I'd had more than the tea and herbal supplements. Or maybe it was reacting to the thought of a supposed serial killer roaming the streets of my hometown. Regardless, I waved, all the while cursing the cat under my breath.

The streets were mostly deserted, the majority of shops along the way having closed hours ago. Brave folks were few and far between in the drizzly darkness. "The perfect night for a murder," I huffed as I shone the beam under bushes and up into skeletal tree branches. With Halloween only a week out, this grim reaper character fit right in. Store owners and groups of students had been donning costumes since the beginning of September. The killer was taking full advantage of the time of year to get away with stalking inno-cent women.

At the corner, cold drops fell from an ancient oak, striking my face and making me flinch. Glancing both ways before crossing the street, I shivered and called to the cat.

Boozy's Bar and Grill still had lights on and a lone male figure sat at an outside table. The sickly yellow glow from the outdoor burners partially illuminated his black hair, short on the sides and longer on top. Magazine-perfect waves hung over his forehead, accenting a handsome face. He wore a wool trench coat, a tie peeking out at the top, and the glass of wine in front of him looked untouched, although his fingerless gloves showed off well-manicured nails. His attention was a million miles away, his body still as stone as he stared at the beverage.

No grim costume. That was good.

As though he felt my gaze, he raised his attention to me. His irises appeared violet and a cold power radiated off him.

I swallowed hard. Those eyes...had to be a trick of the light, right? Instinct and something akin to preservation made me pick up my pace. As I passed the last of the burners, I saw a woman standing in the shadows, watching him. Her features were mostly hidden, but I swear she was smiling. Was she meeting him? Stalking him?

None of my beeswax. She paid no attention to me and I kept walking.

Another approached, heels clacking on the sidewalk. Her skirt stopped well above her knees and the boots she wore jingled, metal embellishments flashing. "Hey," she said. "Chloe, right? That chem test was murder last week, wasn't it?"

Her face was slightly familiar. My memory is great with facts about animal biology, injury protocols, and medical interventions, but I can't remember names. School talk to the rescue. "Totally." Had I turned into a Valley Girl? "Chemistry isn't my favorite."

She made a disgusted face, and something about the action triggered my memory. "You headed to O'Malley's? Three-for-one on beers."

Her name flitted around in my head, and I could almost grasp it. *Barbie? Billie?* I nodded, as though it sounded like a great time. Cheap drinks, drunk college students, and mind numbing small talk. What could be better? Thankfully, I had an excuse. "I'm searching for my landlady's cat. You didn't happen to see any wayward gray tabbies, did you?"

"No, but you have to come to the parade. Everyone will be there."

"Parade?"

Her head tilt suggested I was missing a few screws. "Over on King Street for the Fall Fest." This was said with a mixture of *duh* at me not knowing and anticipation at what I could only guess was another reason to get hammered. "I'm meeting Larson and we're going to watch from the balcony of his dad's shop. Then we're going to O'Malley's."

Shifting to look around her, I scanned the area for Miss Pickles. "Sounds fun. Enjoy."

A pouty face was her response. "You'll come by after you find the cat?"

Why she cared was beyond me, but I nodded with fake enthusiasm. "You had me at three-for-one beers."

She gave a squeal and jumped up and down. "I want you on my team for the trivia game."

Her motive became clearer. "Why is that?"

Another *duh* expression flitted over her features. "You're the smartest girl in school."

Her skirt flipped up as she trotted off to find Larson, whoever that was, and I shook my head, watching her for a moment. No worries about her future. She probably didn't work two jobs to support herself, and a Friday night getting drunk was a highlight in her college career. I wondered what that was like as I watched her bounce away.

As she neared the outdoor dining area of the bar, she turned back. "Hey, do you tutor?"

"No," I called a bit too quickly, trepidation rippling under my skin as I noticed the man at the table observing the interaction. Annoyance and brooding radiated off him in waves. The woman who'd been in the shadows had disappeared.

Darcy. Her name popped into my mind as clear as if he'd spoken it. I swear it had the faintest of accents. *Her name is Darcy Haynes.*

My jaw dropped as I stared at him. Was he in my head? How did *he* know it?

A chill raced down my back. She was still walking, only backwards, and not paying attention to where she was headed—which was right into his table. "I love the parties at O'Malley's."

"Look out!" I yelled.

One of his hands twitched and a gust of wind caught her, her body suddenly shifting away from him. She yelped, but managed to totally miss the table, stumbling slightly. She glanced around, confused. Righting herself, she brushed at her skirt, and gave an embarrassed laugh. "Hey, handsome."

The man zeroed in on his wine glass once more, long fingers stroking the stem absentmindedly. He paid no more attention to her than he would a fly.

Which was good. "You better get going," I told her. "Don't want to be late."

Recovered, she waved at me. "Come find me when you get there!"

Feeling my stare once more, the man pointedly raised his gaze and met mine. His eyes now appeared like dark pools of chocolate in the shadows, the yellowish light a halo at his back. His cheekbones were distinguished, and he took my measure as swiftly as I did his.

While I offered a hesitant smile, he dismissed me as quickly and easily as he had her.

Okay then. Pivoting, I shook it off. I was tired and hungry and wanted to get back home. Jogging the last bit to the park, I touched the can of pepper spray in my pocket to reassure myself, then juggled the flashlight as I scanned the area with the beam.

Miss Pickles loved to sit at the top of the slide like a

lioness surveying her kingdom. I skirted the jungle gym and flooded the slide with illumination, heart sinking when she wasn't there.

The park was divided into thirds, a children's area at the east end with playground equipment and a small soccer field. The middle and largest section offered a basketball court and little league ballfield. The far west, tennis courts. A paved track encircled the entire thing, and overhead solar lights burned here and there, most of them nonfunctioning, as I trudged through the open grass. The blades were wet and sparkled when my light cruised over them.

Four teenage boys played pick up and I asked if they'd seen the cat. No dice, and I continued my search, methodically moving east to west.

An older woman walked a dog on the track, although the park had signs posted banning canines. Headphones in and busy texting, she paid no heed to her bully mix fascinated by odors off the paved way. He probably had some hound in him by the look of his tail and ears, and his nose was on the ground, sniffing incessantly. At one point, he stopped abruptly at the edge of a ditch between the path and subdivision on the other side, causing her to stumble. She called him, tugged on the leash, all the while texting, although Rebel refused to budge. Apparently, he was living up to his name.

Incensed, she pocketed the phone and got the dog's attention by pulling out a treat. He loped over, devoured the bribe, and off they went.

"Miss Pickles?" I called softly into the overgrowth of the ditch near the short wooden bridge that linked the subdivision to the park. I opened the tuna pack and waved it in the air in front of me.

The scent was as likely to draw a raccoon, or heaven

forbid, a bear. I prayed it would only capture her attention, but I was ready to call it quits, thinking about my nice warm bed. I couldn't stand the thought of her being out here, though, or Vera's grief if I didn't bring her favorite cat home.

In the distance, I heard a cheer go up and a band begin playing an upbeat march. The parade was kicking off.

"I should be out having fun," I groused to the MIA cat, sinking down in a crouch and rattling the foil pack. "I'm young and it's Friday night. But what am I doing? Saying no to invitations to go out with friends and stalking through drizzling rain to save you from yourself."

A soft meow issued from the ditch and out crawled a drenched and dirty gray tabby.

"Well, aren't you a mess?"

A bit of coaxing and I scooped her up, letting her eat from my hand. She resisted for a moment, but gave in, too wet and tired to put up a fight.

I hurried out of the park, the flashlight beam bouncing around as we went. "Which boy toy did you have your way with tonight?" I teased.

My eyes automatically searched for the man at the bar and grill, but he was gone. I breathed a sigh of relief and hustled past the place, now dark.

I was still dreaming of my bed when I felt Miss Pickles tense and the hair on the back of my neck stood at attention. I started to pick up my pace, my tired legs be damned, when a woman's scream cut through the night.

It sounded an awful lot like Darcy.

THREE

The sound had come from up ahead. My foot slid on a greasy spot on the sidewalk as I ran, nearly causing me to tumble over myself with the cat. I dropped the flashlight instead, and it went skidding off to the side. Regaining my balance and retrieving it, I sprinted on.

"Darcy?" I shouted, shifting Miss Pickles to dig out my phone and dial nine-one-one. I overrode the operator and simply told her a woman was being assaulted near the Blooms & Petals florist shop.

As I approached the opening to the alley, I heard muffled cries. "Please don't. I'm not ready! I'm only twenty-one! No...."

As Miss Pickles and I rounded the corner, I skidded to a stop. Deep shadows and a rising fog enveloped the narrow strip of brick walls between the florist and the neighboring building. A disgusting odor, like old, cut flowers left in water too long wafted toward me.

"Help!" Darcy screamed, and I fumbled with the flashlight to shine the beam into the foggy darkness.

A tall figure dressed in long, flowing robes towered over

her. She pressed herself against the wet wall as hard as she could. As the illumination hit them, they both glanced in my direction, startled, and the beam glinted off a huge curved blade in the robed man's hand.

The serial killer! My teeth chattered and the frosty fog seemed to seep into my bones. I swallowed the fear jamming up my throat. "The Halloween parade is on King Street, moron," I yelled, hoping my voice might raise other people's suspicion. "Leave her alone."

His face was covered with a partial mask, the eyes seeming to be black rimmed and the cheekbones skeletal. He cocked his head at me and his real mouth moved in an evil smile. "Two for one tonight."

Miss Pickles hissed. Darcy thrashed, seemingly pinned to the bricks by invisible hands. "Chloe! Help me! He's going to kill me!"

I shook the flashlight and attempted to reach for my pepper spray, but the fat cat was seriously hampering my rescue abilities, not to mention the mind tingling cold and fear gripping my insides. "Just come over here, Darcy."

"I can't," she whined. "My legs won't move."

Had he drugged her? How was she still standing?

Yanking out the spray, I unceremoniously squeezed Miss Pickles inside my coat, zipping her in and switching on my headlamp. The beam wasn't as strong as the flashlight, but caught the tall man's ugly... Wait, were those *fangs?* "Dude, are you a grim reaper or a vampire? You seem to have identity confusion." My bravado did not totally conceal my fear. I took a step sideways, hoping to distract him, and the cat meowed. *Follow me, big guy.* "I already called the cops. You better get out of here while you can."

He laughed, the sound like fingernails on a chalkboard. It raked across my chest, icy hot. Exposing the fangs that looked extremely lifelike, he snapped them at me. Self-preservation kicked in and I stepped back automatically. The eerie timber of his voice echoed between the walls. "Come closer."

Yeah, right! "Fat chance. You come with me."

Before I could blink, he was in front of me, his weapon raised. I screamed, Miss Pickles launched from my coat, scratching me deep, and I smacked the guy in the rib cage with the flashlight.

The blow was weak, but the cat landed on him, knocking him off kilter. The blade clanged against a dumpster as his feet tangled and he pitched awkwardly to the left.

The echo rang in my ears. Was that thing real? *Get a grip*. Of course, it was. This was no amateur in a Halloween costume. If he truly was the serial killer, I was dead.

As he regained his balance, he shot out a hand toward me. I yelped and jumped, my shoes slipping on the wet asphalt. Flailing and thrashing to remain upright, I fumbled with the pepper spray.

My trembling fingers dropped the canister. It landed in a puddle of who knew what. I dove for it as he reached for me again. His hand caught the ends of my hair.

He yanked. My head jerked to the side and the cat again intervened, planting herself in front of his feet. He was in mid-stride to shove me against the bricks, but fell over her, taking me to the ground with him.

His heavy weight forced air from my lungs, my scream turning to a muffled "*oof*."

Thunder boomed overhead, the cloying smell of dead roses and wet soil intensifying. The combined odors took me immediately back to my parents' funeral. Sickness enveloped me and my stomach revolted. The black garb he wore fell over my eyes, blinding me, and claustrophobia instantly set in. I vaguely heard Darcy yell something, followed by the *clip-clop* of her heels running away.

Some friend she was.

The man stood, allowing me to breathe once more. He shouted a curse in a language I didn't recognize.

Get up, some part of my rational mind shouted, *or you'll be dead!*

My muscles responded, the memory of losing my parents mixed in with this frightening encounter. I crawled to my feet, seeing my attacker peering around the alley corner. Darcy was no longer in sight.

At least she got away. I fought through the cloying contraction of my lungs, my nose burning. Miss Pickles screeched, and I scrambled to grab the pepper spray. Where was the flashlight? Clouds covered the moon and rain fell in earnest. I could barely see my own hands in the chilly fog.

"You cost me her soul," the man growled, and I whirled to find him right behind me.

He hit me with an open palm to the temple. The blow was so hard, it sent me flying into the florist's wall. My body was no match for the bricks, and everything from my brain to my internal organs slammed to the right before ricocheting from the impact. I crumpled to the ground, gasping, and that distant, rational part of my mind screamed silently in terror.

I knew without a doubt, he was going to kill me.

FOUR

The edge of the blade gleamed in the light of my headlamp. The strap had broken, thanks to the slam against the wall, and the contraption lay a few feet away, spotlighting us with its weak beam.

Ears ringing, I moved on instinct, lunging for the handle of the weapon. The reaper's boot caught me in the ribs, fiery hot pain exploding in my side and rippling into my back. I flipped over, not even enough breath in my lungs to cry, and my fingers glided across the wet grip.

Dragging myself away from him, I tried a second time, everything in me screaming. With adrenaline-fueled strength, I catapulted forward, my chest landing on the compact scythe. I rolled onto my right side, hugging it to me, but before I could rise, his boney fingers gripped me around my throat. He lifted me high, my feet dangling, and I suddenly had to fight for oxygen all over again.

This guy's workout must be something. The thought almost made me laugh, the whole thing so *not* funny, his strength seemingly superhuman. But I still had his knife. It was awkward, though not as heavy as I had imagined, and I nearly dropped it, yet managed to hang on. Stars flickered at the edge of my vision, the fog creeping closer. Malice coated what features I could see of his face as he pinned me against the wall and leaned in.

I caught the stench of death. My free hand clawed at his hold and I used what little force I had to kick him. I landed a knee to his groin, but he barely flinched. His fangs seemed to grow longer, or was my oxygen-deprived brain imagining it?

For a beat, I closed my eyes and prayed. *This is all a nightmare, a hallucination.* The guru's tea and supplements had brought this on. I'd wake up any minute now...

The crushing pressure on my windpipe argued the point. *Don't die!* If you died in a dream, you died for real—wasn't that what they claimed?

My face pivoted to the right against my will. The points of his teeth scratched their way down my neck. My eyes flew open and I screamed, the sound ragged but enough to bounce around the alley.

The reaper laughed, stepping back and yet maintaining his vise grip on my throat. "You're a hellcat," he said with what sounded like begrudging approval. "Don't worry, I'm going after your friend as soon as I'm done with you."

Anger at him roared through me, numbing the pain. The weapon felt light as a feather now, and before I could suck in another breath, it seemed to lift my hand into the air.

Kill.

It was either him or me, but the voice in my head had materialized out of nowhere. It wasn't mine, and it didn't have the accent I'd heard previously.

Didn't matter. What choice did I have? I had to fight.

I swung with all my might, a raw scream ripping from

my damaged throat. The blade hit with force...and then bounced off the black robes.

Another laugh from him rattled around in my bones. My vision swam, becoming a tunnel with dancing stars outlining it.

Swing it again, the voice instructed.

My limbs hung like a rag doll's, the fight winking out of me. I felt detached, the anger still burning but my body not responding.

My muffled hearing caught the sound of Miss Pickles' meow. My landlady's face flashed across my mind. Nita's, too. My aunt and uncle.

My parents.

All the things I hadn't done in my twenty-four years filled me up, squeezing me. All the dreams I hadn't fulfilled, the promises I hadn't kept.

The monster's eyes and bared teeth were so close to my face, revulsion made me tremble. His fangs left my neck long enough for him to command, "Look at me." I flicked my gaze toward his, holding my breath against his reeking stench. "That's right, I want to see the life leave your eyes when I kill you."

As if it had a will of its own, my arm raised the curved blade. It felt as though a giant hand were assisting me, the scythe once again easy to swing.

This time, I raised it a foot higher. *This* time, I swung with every last ounce of energy I had.

Schick.

Like a hot knife through butter, it cut through his neck quickly. For a heartbeat nothing changed, except my fingers losing their ability to hold onto the handle.

His eyes lost focus and turned glassy. The chokehold on

my throat went flaccid. Whatever pinned me to the wall instantly fled.

His body toppled.

My feet hit first, but stamina had long since fled my limbs, and I, too, went down in a heap. As I gasped for air that couldn't get past my injured trachea, my vision shrank to a lone spot.

The man's head, neatly severed from his body, lay on the wet ground staring back at me.

FIVE

Floating several feet, I gawked at the awful scene. The rain continued to fall, the thick fog and gray shadows doing a mysterious dance. The headless man and my body lay side by side unmoving. A frozen tableau in the dirty, dripping alley.

Miss Pickles hid under an empty wooden crate near the dumpster. My headlamp, flashlight, and pepper spray were scattered around. While I'd thought the scythe had fallen to my left, it now lay near me, as if still defending me in death from its owner.

I felt no pain; my floating spirit seemed opaque. My hands and fingers appeared a filmy white in front of my face as I examined them. Freaking out, I patted my torso, my hands feeling no resistance and disappearing into the diaphanous matter.

A string tightened around my chest, tugging me up and away. "No, no, *no*." My voice was nothing but an echo in my ears. "This can't be happening."

I fought the magnetic draw and attempted to force my

spirit back into its physical container lying motionless on the ground.

"No, wait," I heard a voice say, and I turned to see another spirit floating up above the buildings. My attacker, without his costume. "I can't die!" he screamed, nothing more than a grayish phantom. "It's not my time. My contract isn't—"

Poof, he winked out like a dead firework.

"It's not your time, either, Chloe bear."

I whirled, searching for the owner of the voice. My heart thudded hard in my chest. "Mom?"

"You may be tempted to cross over," she continued, "but you have work to do here. Fight, sweetie. For me."

From the end of the alley, quickly moving footsteps sounded on the damp pavement. I said her name again, still searching for her, but she didn't answer.

The footsteps had grown silent. I pivoted, my astral body nearly somersaulting at the lack of gravity and the sudden motion. "Darcy?"

The form that emerged wasn't my beer-drinking friend. A new sensation entered my chest as the man from Boozy's glanced at me hovering above my body. His gaze dropped to the lifeless form, and he cursed under his breath and wiped his eyes. "*Doamne.*" I had no idea what that meant, but it had the same accent as the voice I'd heard inside my head earlier . "We have quite the situation, don't we?"

"Wait." I tried to propel myself toward him and ended up facing the wall. I put up my hands to push off it, but they went through the bricks. I looked over my shoulder. "You can see me?"

He didn't answer, examining my attacker's beheaded corpse.

"It was you, wasn't it? I heard you tell me Darcy's name."

He sized up the alley and the man. With a slight look of disbelief, he shook his head. Or maybe it was distaste. "You are fearless, I'll give you that. Foolish, but brave."

"Foolish? I just saved my friend."

"And caused your own demise," he countered.

"Wait... I'm..." I struggled to say the word, even though I knew it was true. "Dead?"

His eyes seemed violet again as the silvery light caught in them. "Close enough."

The blade on the ground tremored and I blinked. He hadn't touched it. "Who are you? Are you a doctor?" *Please be a doctor.*

"No, but I will save you." As I watched in horror, he pulled back his lips and bit his own wrist. Blood welled.

"Gross!" My uncooperative form floated a few feet away, but at least I was facing him again. Might have been better if I hadn't—he dripped the red substance onto my lips, forcing my slack mouth open. "Dude, not cool!"

"This will sustain you."

What kind of freak was he?

No good deed goes unpunished, I told myself. This is what I got for helping Vera.

Sirens echoed in the night, drawing close. Where had they been all this time?

"We must hurry." He placed his other hand over my damaged larynx, and all of a sudden, I felt stronger in my ghostly form. The tugging in my chest lessened.

He closed his eyes, blood continuing to drip into my mouth from his open wound. A faint glow enveloped my throat. Enveloped him.

I wasn't sure I could freak out more, but that's where I

was headed—the top of the scale, whatever that was. "Stop," I demanded, attempting to push him away. My hand went through his shoulder. "The police are coming. They'll give me CPR and call an ambulance."

"They cannot resurrect you. Now, be quiet. I need to concentrate."

All my pushing and shoving did no good. "Look, I don't know who you are or what kind of aberrant stuff you're into..."

"Aberrant?" The corner of his mouth twitched. Oh, he was amused, was he? He removed his hand and I watched as his cut wrist stopped bleeding instantaneously and appeared to seal itself. "Get in your body."

I blinked a couple times and shook my head, trying to clear the image of his skin healing. "I really wish I hadn't taken those supplements." This had to be a drug-induced trip. Had. To. Be. "I've already tried that," I told him. "It didn't work."

"You're stronger now." He stood and pointed at my prone form. "Do it."

I don't like being ordered around, but I was desperate. No way was I dying tonight. Whatever trip this was, I was in control.

At least, that's what I told myself.

I concentrated, and my spirit moved closer. My brain gave up a 'hallelujah,' and I focused harder. Staring down at my broken shell, I willed myself to merge with it. "Come on," I muttered.

Nothing happened.

I squeezed my eyes shut and tried again.

"You have to want it," the man said.

"I do!" Nothing happened. I peeked open an eyelid. For days, weeks, after my parents died, I couldn't get out of bed.

I'd wanted to join them. Now, I fought against it with all my might. "I want to live!" I shouted.

A new sensation latched onto me, seemingly attached to my spirit like a cord. I could see it, silvery and shiny, running from my physical chest to my ghostly one. "I think it's working."

The siren was nearly on top of us. "Hurry."

I squeezed my eyes shut again and imagined reeling my spirit into my body using the cord. The floaty sensation wore off. Opening my eyes, I saw I was moving toward my lifeless self. A wave of relief rippled through me. "It's working!" At the same time, the dead man shuddered, as if he, too, were coming back to life. "What's happening?"

As we both watched, he thankfully didn't resurrect. Instead, his corpse made a slight popping sound and turned to what resembled sawdust. I stared, clinging to my physical form and hoping I didn't do the same. With a second, distinct pop, his head followed.

"Holy moly." The cord tugged harder, undeniable now. My spirit twitched and cramped, and I wondered what new hell this was. A second later, I snapped, rather than popped, back into my container.

Gazing upward, I saw clouds skitter across the slice of sky overhead. My attacker's cloak rose, as though draped on a ghost, and hovered near me. The weapon slid onto my chest, the handle slipping into my grip.

"This is unprecedented," the violet-eyed man said in a hushed tone.

The handle was hot and trembled in my fingers. "What is?"

The cloak fell on me, blotting out my view. A searing white light followed, and I felt my spirit and body reconnect totally and completely. My stomach flipped and my lungs screamed for air. I gasped for oxygen, the sweet sensation of the life-giving element flowing down my damaged throat.

I'm alive! The rush was heady, a tickling sensation flooding my limbs. Even though the disgusting black robes covered me, I welcomed their stink of death.

I was about to yank the fabric off and sit up when the light whited out my vision. Before I could draw another breath, I was pitched from it into absolute darkness.

SIX

I woke to the sound of a cat coughing up a hairball.

Sitting up so fast I nearly gave myself whiplash, I gasped in a lungful of air and blinked at the collection of cut flower arrangements surrounding the spot where I lay.

The cat gagged again and flowing dark material tangled around my ankles when I tried to gain my feet and find her. There is absolutely nothing like a pet vomiting to bring you out of a nearly dead state and back to full consciousness before you can even open your eyes.

My belongings were lined up in a neat row on the bottom shelf of a wooden counter, the strange man seated with his back against it. The compact scythe was propped near a stool.

"Sit down," he said evenly.

Outside the building, I heard the crackle of a police radio. A strobing blue light rhythmically swept through the shop. I glanced around wildly, taking in the flowers and the large front display window. "Did you break in here?"

"Lower your voice," he commanded, giving me a quelling look. "They'll depart in a minute."

"But I have to tell them—eep!" I was suddenly on my butt facing him.

"Tell them what exactly?" He held my gaze with steady fortitude. "That you killed a grim reaper? What will you say when they ask about the body?"

"I'll tell them..." I stopped, remembering the pop, the sawdust. The truth was so farfetched, even I didn't believe it. "I... Was that... I mean, that man—was he a serial killer?"

An officer's voice outside made Violet Eyes glare and motion for me to be quiet. His words came out a whisper. "He was a rogue grim, and a vampire to boot. No scruples. You did me a favor, however prodigious your actions. I need a moment to figure out our next move."

Our next move? Vampire? Once more, I started to rise, the cloak making me itch. "I'm going home and getting some sleep. When I wake up, this will be a bad dream, nothing more. This is a hallucination brought on by sleep deprivation and a bad combo of natural"—I made air quotes—"supplements."

Again, some type of invisible force grasped hold of me and jerked me down. *He* was doing this. That's why Darcy had avoided falling into his table. But how?

He spoke through gritted teeth, authority radiating off him in coiling waves. "You exterminated a grim, something I've never encountered with a mundane. The rules are absolute; you must wear the robes for a year. At that time, you may choose to turn them in or continue your service to Soul Management Group."

"The what what?" Talk about mad as a hatter. Miss Pickles appeared, wrapping her feline body around the corner of the counter and gliding over to him. She seemed okay and I breathed a sigh of relief. He scratched under her chin and she purred. Dumb cat. "That man out there"—I hitched a thumb toward the alley—"was a killer, I'll give you that, but he was dressed as a reaper, because that's his MO. Don't you watch the news? It's nearly Halloween and he could blend in with all the parade folks on King Street."

He started to reply, but checked himself, angling his face slightly. Had he caught the sound of something outside? I mimicked him, but couldn't hear a thing.

Then it came. I was so tense, I jumped when one of the officers jiggled the door handle. I involuntarily started to yelp when Violet Eyes waved a hand, creating a breeze on my face. The weighted force held me down, restraining any sound and my breath.

Reapers, vampires, invisible hands... Maybe my therapist was right, I was subconsciously holding onto things I needed to get rid of. If I didn't, I was headed to the looney bin.

I swore mentally, now more terrified of the man than the police. The officer moved and the restriction around my throat eased. I coughed and judged how fast I could grab the weapon, and...

He held a finger to his lips and I heard the cop call to a partner, telling him they were wasting their time. A moment later, the blue light shut off and we heard the cruiser leave.

Absolute silence fell in the shop, except for the cat's purring. I was shaking and cold to the bone. I needed to get away from this guy and fast. Needed to get my bearings. *Sleep.* Everything would make sense in the light of morning. "I'll ask you again, who are you?" My throat felt fine, but my whispered tone shook with fear. "*What* are you?"

"I am the one who saved your life," he said flatly.

I was grateful for that. Grateful the cat was okay, too. But nothing else about this night was normal and my flight or fight instincts were kicking in so hard I was vibrating. Flight was definitely my choice.

He must have sensed my panic. Easing forward, he locked eyes with me. "You are safe. Take a deep breath through the nose and let it out through your mouth."

Riggght. He was going to school me on how to control a pending anxiety attack? The absurdity made me laugh. "Please tell me you don't have any diseases."

His features were less visible without the strobing effect. "Mundanes." He shook his head. "The things you worry about."

Would my legs hold me if I needed to run? "You put blood in my mouth. I can't tell you how disgusting that is. You're a total stranger, and a weird-as-hell one at that. Even in my wildest days, I didn't let a boy kiss me until I knew his name."

Nothing changed in his expression. "In order to save your life, I shared blood with you, and if it makes you feel better, my name is Killion."

The name reverberated through me like he'd struck a bass drum in my chest. My nerves, already fried, tingled. A pregnant pause fell. He waited, patient. Under his intense scrutiny, I wanted to fidget.

I didn't. "I may not be a doctor, but last I checked, blood is not a miracle cure."

So still and unmoving, he waited another long moment before answering and every cell I possessed went on edge. If I could've ran out the door screaming, I might have. My lizard brain insisted he was the thing of horror movies. Of nightmares. "I am immune to human illness and disease."

I shook my head, trying to remove the memory of his teeth biting into his own skin. Throat tight, I forced myself to swallow. "Okay, then." I was able to rise, the force no longer keeping me down. I peeled off the robe and let it puddle at my feet. The scythe trembled in its spot. Ignoring both it and him, I pointed at the cat, who had climbed into his lap. "It's been fun and all, but it's time for me to get Miss Pickles home."

"While I present no threat to you, Gustafson's group does."

My brain felt like it had a short. "Who's Gustafson?"

"The rogue grim you terminated. His followers will attempt to avenge his death, and while most are non-magical, they use blood to power spells. Because of your reaper status combined with my blood, you'll be harder to kill, but you're not immortal."

Reaper status. *Yeah, so not going there.* Hands trembling, I scooped up my belongings, including the cat. She complained loudly as I removed her from Killion's lap. I took a step back, putting distance between us. "You need help. This delusion of yours is out of control."

The weapon fell over and slid on its own accord toward me. I jumped away. "Stop that. Whatever you're doing, just stop it."

His gaze was fixed, and while his face was stone, a hint of glittering amusement shone in those eyes. Was this some sort of sick game to him? "After all you've witnessed, it seems *you're* the delusional one. A certain period of denial is to be expected after a near-death experience, but you cannot escape the repercussions. The robes chose you, Chloe. You are now a grim reaper, whether you like it or not."

SEVEN

How did he know my name?

His words rang in my ears all the way home. I didn't bring an ID and Darcy had never said my name out loud.

I tried to ignore his voice floating around in my head but found myself talking out loud to Miss Pickles and sounding as unhinged as I felt. "Could grim reapers be real?" The rain had stopped and the cat blinked up at me from the cradle of my arms. As I hurried down the sidewalk, I scratched the top of her head. "Did I actually kill one?"

The parade had ended. Adults with kids in costumes and drunken revelers dotted the street. Someone called out a greeting, but I didn't recognize him, and my brain was occupied with other things.

"What does that mean—*the robes chose you?*" I mimicked Killion's deep voice, although the accent wasn't right. "And did you see the incisors on Gustafson? They looked three shades of real. If there *are* grims, maybe there are vampires, too?"

A shiver ran up the back of my neck from the memory

of those fangs against my throat. Up ahead, a threesome of staggering, boisterous guys blocked the sidewalk. They joked and hooted, smacking each other in the arms with fake punches. "Hello, beautiful," said the tall, skinny one who sported a shaggy goatee.

I debated going around them, but I'd had a lousy night and their mere presence pissed me off. My feet were already soaked and I didn't relish wading through the drenched grass. "Move."

Expecting resistance, or at least an argument, I was shocked when they all froze and something changed in their eyes. The streetlamp overhead flickered. "Uhh, sure," Goatee said. "No problem." He shifted aside and the other two lined up like soldiers behind him to let me pass.

Once we were several feet away, I murmured to the cat, "That was weird."

Miss Pickles purred. As we neared the apartment, her owner—obviously waiting for us—flung open the door and rushed out to meet us. "My baby!" Vera hefted the cat from my arms, smothered her in kisses, and squeezed her so tight the poor animal's eyes bugged out. "Thank you for saving her," she cooed. "Give Chloe a kiss!"

Accepting the cat's face shoved into mine, I assured her it was no problem before I trudged up the stairs to my place amid more thanks and an offer to take thirty dollars off the coming month's rent. I assured Vera that was appreciated but not necessary. Then I closed myself inside my apartment and fell face first into bed.

THE ALARM BLARED at five and I moaned, fumbling in the sheets to turn it off. I was warm and sleepy and the intrusion was unwelcome. Slapping the snooze button, I curled deeper into the blanket until an unwelcome odor hit my nose.

I sat up, throwing off the covers. "What in the world?"

Unfortunately, the odor was coming from me. The previous night's excursion came crashing back and I grabbed my head with both hands, trying to stop the flood of memories.

I killed a grim reaper. Whether it was a supernatural one, as Killion had tried to convince me of, or the maggot of a human being who'd been murdering innocent woman, was yet to be determined.

While my brain played whack-a-mole with images, I forced myself from bed. My backup alarm on my phone buzzed incessantly inside my purse on the chair. I clamored to locate the thing amongst the hoard of items and turned it off. Doing so, I saw I'd missed multiple texts from Nita.

Ignoring those, I yanked my work uniform from the clothes basket and sniffed. I hadn't done laundry, but it would have to do. I pressed at the wrinkles with my hands, which was pointless, and gave up to stumble into the shower. For someone who had died and come back to life, I felt okay. I didn't seem to have any injuries, and I'd slept nearly seven hours. A record these days.

I wanted to linger in the gentle cascade of water, but I couldn't be late to open the shop. Focusing on getting ready kept me distracted enough I could forget about last night.

Vera was waiting as I rushed down the outside staircase, her hair still in plastic curlers. Miss Pickles was doing circle eights around her ankles, and she shoved a sandwich baggie at me. "Toasted bagel with strawberry cream cheese, just the way you like it."

I thanked her, patted the cat, and took off down the dark, quiet morning street.

EIGHT

The smell of ground coffee is one of my favorite things in the whole world. It never fails to put me in a good mood.

I had the machines warmed and a pan of muffins baking when Nita arrived to unlock the front door and start taking orders.

"Are you blowing me off, Frost?" She hung her coat in the backroom and pulled on an apron.

Since I was rinsing a frosting bucket in the deep stainless steel sink, I wasn't sure I'd heard her correctly over the noise. I shot her a quizzical look as I shut off the water. "What?"

"I texted you a dozen times last night." Her face was a mask of worry. "Did you even read them?"

"Blame it on your tea and supplements." I know *I* was still trying to. "I slept like the dead." The irony hit me after the words were out of my mouth, and a begrudging smile passed my lips.

"You did?" Her annoyance turned to glee. "Told you they'd work."

A line of regulars was lined up outside. The moment she flipped the sign, we went to work. The next few hours were filled with drink orders and hoping there would be some form of sweet confections left over at break time. The routine did me good, although I went on high alert when I heard Officer Pete Rogan's voice at the counter. After he'd ordered his usual triple espresso and toasted almond scone, he asked Nita, "Everything normal when you got here this morning?"

"Yeah, I think so. But I didn't arrive until six." She called to me over her shoulder, and I felt more than saw her odd expression. "Chloe?"

I kept my head down. "Perfectly fine. Why?"

The leather of his holster creaked as he put a casual hand on the weapon. "Night patrol got a call about a disturbance in the alley next to the flower shop. Dave and I are following up with all the businesses in a three block area this morning."

Nita had a slight crush on the officer, and I heard her flirty voice engage. "What kind of disturbance? Like a break-in?"

She sounded entirely too excited about the prospect.

I hit the grinder, drowning them out, then tamped the grounds for the drink I was building.

Pete called to me once it was finished. "You sure you didn't notice anything unusual this morning?"

I shook my head, still not looking in his direction. "Not a thing."

He and Nita chatted a bit longer. He took his drink and bag. "Call if you discover anything amiss."

"You know I will," she told him. "Here, take this cookie to your partner." She handed him another bag with the treat inside. "We so appreciate all you do to keep the neighbor-hood safe."

I tried not to make gagging noises as I pushed the button on the espresso machine and listened to it click in. Beautiful dark liquid flowed into the diner cup I held under it.

For the next hour, she rang up customers while I built drinks. In between rushes, she complained about her ex who wanted to get back together, and her fantasies about Officer Rogan. I fell into the ebb and flow of the job, bussing tables when not behind the counter.

During my first break, Nita stuck her head into the backroom. "Hey, there's a guy here to see you."

I froze with a bite of half-eaten bagel in my mouth, and hurriedly swallowed. "Who is it?"

She shrugged. "Skinny guy, sounds British."

Curious, I stood and crinkled my napkin. That description ruled out anyone I knew, including the mysterious Killion.

Nita entered, letting the swinging double doors slap closed behind her. Shoulder to shoulder, we peeked out the oval window of one. As described, the guy leaning on the far end of the counter was thin, well over six feet tall, and appeared young under several layers of clothes. His outer wool coat was threadbare in places, and he wore a news-paper boy hat cocked sideways on his head. His eyes darted around the shop in a nervous gesture, and his hand rested on an enormously thick book with straps holding it shut.

"I have no idea who that is."

"He said he needed to conduct business with you," she murmured. "Do you think it's about one of Velma's dogs? Maybe he wants to adopt."

While Vera collected cats, her sister ran a dog rescue. Helping Paws often called on my vet tech skills to keep the animals healthy. "Maybe." Something told me not. "Stay here."

"Why? What's wrong?"

My friend was entirely too curious for her own good. "Nothing. Can you put a fresh batch of cookies in?"

"You've been moping around like Wednesday Addams all morning, and now this? What aren't you telling me?"

"Nothing, but we do need cookies for the lunch crowd." I gave her my best smile. I outranked her by seniority and the fact I was the owner's favorite, since he used to take his huskies to my parents' clinic.

"Fine," she relented, going to the sink to wash her hands. "But I really think you need to get out more. The morgue is turning you into a zombie."

I pushed through the door and faced the man. "Can I help you?"

"Blimey." He looked me over with a frown. "You're the one who took out 281?"

"What are you talking about?"

On closer inspection, I noticed a crooked front tooth and some barely-there facial hair. "Gustafson. The grim you"—he made a slashing motion across his throat.

Two elderly ladies at the side table gasped. They exchanged a shocked look, and I hastily motioned for him to keep his voice down. "How do you know about that?" I whispered.

He acted taken aback. "Killion. Who do you think reported it to SMG?" The book wiggled on the countertop under his hand, and I eyed it warily. The buckles unlocked on their own and the ladies gasped again. "I can't believe the robes chose someone like you. Anyway, place your thumb on line three."

The book flew open, pages flipping like a fan was

blowing them. Abruptly, they stopped, falling open to reveal names. Along with them were numbers and fingerprints.

Under the gaze of the old ladies, I stifled a groan and gave them a wink. "Cool trick, right? He's practicing for his magic act." I drew him and the book around to the very end of the countertop and blocked their view. "What is that?" I pointed at the open volume.

"Don't you know nothin'? This is the book of soul collectors, like you, Grave Girl. You reap the non-compliants. Thumb, please." He grabbed my hand, and although I wrestled and resisted, it was drawn to him and completely uncontrollable.

Nita burst from the backroom. "Hey, what's going on? Let go of her."

I held up my other hand and shifted my body to block her line of sight. "It's okay. Really. He's my...cousin. From...London."

Frowning, she eyed us suspiciously. "You never told me you had a cousin in London."

"Yep, this is him." I whacked him on the arm. He flinched. "He's leaving to go back today."

"Can't wait to get out of here," he said, looking at her, but I was pretty sure he was speaking to me.

She wasn't buying it, but the shop's phone rang. "We'll talk about this later," she informed me.

Once she was busy, I wheeled on the man. He still held my hand in a steel grip. "What are you doing?"

"Hold still."

"Ouch," I yelped at the sharp prick of some invisible source that brought blood to my skin. The elderly women leaned over to stare. "What the...?"

My thumb landed on the third line down from the top,

ignoring my resistance. A fiery sensation licked over my fingers and up my arm. Before I could curse, the book released me.

My print, in blood, glowed a devilish red for a bright second, then dried instantly, turning a rusty brown. Still reeling from the fire in my arm, the skin above my left pectoral went tight and a fresh inferno erupted there. "Oh, mamma!" My hand flew to the spot and I gulped. It felt like a giant needle was blazing through the flesh over my heart. "What is going on?"

"Your mark." He pointed to my chest. "All grims get one. The non-magic folks will see a butterfly, but official SMG employees will see your mark and know who you are. Handier than the sigils grims used to have each time they went to harvest a soul."

Cautiously, I lifted my shirt. A skull and bones, with a scythe struck through them, had been tattooed into my skin. "You can't mark people against their will."

"When your reaper gig is up, it will fade."

"Dude, no. Get it off."

"That's not how this works." He brought out a phone and tapped the screen. "What's your email?"

I sucked at my thumb, staring at the bloody print, and wondering how to get out of this. Now, I realized the others were in blood as well, just aged and brown. "I'm not giving you my contact info. I'm not right for this job, and I want this ink gone."

"The Hall of Souls moved into the current century a decade ago," he said, ignoring my demands. "We send employment contracts via email now. Saving trees and all that."

"Contract?" Fighting with the napkin holder closest to me, I tore a sheet free. Nita had stuffed the metal holder entirely too full. I wrapped the thin, white paper around my injury. "Look, there's been a mistake. I don't want to do this."

A roll of his eyes told me he didn't care. "Of course. I understand. It takes some getting use to, but the benefits are nice, right?"

I felt like a parrot, mimicking him. "What benefits?"

"Bloody hell. Did that wanker Killion not tell you anything?"

An alarm began to ring. The book slammed shut all on its own, the two straps closing themselves. The man glanced at an unusual looking watch on his wrist, very steampunk-ish, and shut off the sound. "I'm late. Gotta run, love. It's all outlined in the contract. Now, what's your bloody email?"

In a state of numbness, I rattled it off.

He smiled politely and shoved the cell into a vest pocket. "Very well, then. Welcome to the team, and all that malarkey. Your psychopomp will arrive shortly, you have your robes and the scythe. Good luck, 281."

He snatched up the old book and proceeded to walk out. After a moment's hesitation, I ran after him and caught him at the door. "I thought the dead reaper—Gustafson—was 281."

"Right, and you killed him—quite a feat, that—but good riddance, eh? A real diva and doing shady stuff, he was. You're filling his robes, so you also get his number." Another check of his watch. "Killion can answer any other questions tonight. Remember, you only handle non-compliants from here on out. No reaping those whose life contracts aren't up."

With a hesitant pat on my arm that was really a shove to get me out of the way, he sailed out the door. "I expect free coffee next time, Grave Girl," he called.

I stared at my napkin-wrapped thumb. It didn't hurt any longer. Neither did the skin over my heart.

Nita rushed from the back and stood alongside me, watching him go. "What did he want?"

I peeled off the napkin, now spotless, not a drop of blood anywhere. My wound was gone, too, the skin healed. One of my new benefits?

I laughed from sheer, hopeless fear. This was real.

I'd killed a grim reaper, died myself for two minutes, heard my mom speak to me, and now worked for a group who managed souls. "Nothing," I lied. I peeked another glance at the tattoo. There was no red skin around it like a real one would leave. "Just some follow-up paperwork involving my parents' accident."

Thinking of them, I suddenly had an idea. If I was a reaper, could I commune with the dead? I mean, I'd spoken with my mom when I died, could I open that spirit line again? It was the first thing that made me actually interested in believing what was going on.

My friend's eyes filled with concern. "Go finish your break. I saved you two macadamia muffins. You need sugar. You look like you've seen a ghost."

As I returned to the work room, ignoring the odd looks from the elderly women, I hoped I might actually someday see two of them.

NINE

Sipping a large Baby Bomb Nita put in a to-go cup for me, I took my time walking home. As I did, I read the email from a woman named Mei Han, of the Soul Management Department, welcoming me to the team.

Her precisely worded note assured me that my "watcher" would be in contact within twenty-four hours, and my personal psychopomp would arrive by carrier in that time, as well. The contract was a twenty-two page PDF attachment that I struggled to read, not only because of the formatting but also the terms were alien to me and legal mumbo-jumbo always made me want to poke my eyes out.

Someone banged into my arm, causing my phone to fly from my hand. Only when I glanced up did I realize I had walked into the other person, not him into me.

"Watch it," he muttered.

The tattoo on my chest went fiery hot. *Kill,* I heard that weird voice in my head commence. "Sorry." I scrambled for the device and made a face at the guy's back, not appreciating the curses he said as he continued on. *Not killing him,* I retorted to the scythe, or whatever that voice belonged to.

Pocketing the cell, I simply stood there, my mind reeling. According to what I *had* been able to discern from my new employment contract, my living expenses would be paid. I was entitled to PTO equal to three weeks of vacation, and any injuries occurred on the job that did not "self-heal" would be covered by SMG's health insurance. They even had grants to cover university costs and an incentive program to keep grims re-upping.

Granted, this was all available after a thirty-day probation period, and my contract stated it was for a year beyond that—non-negotiable, according to Section A3.

Vera met me at the door of the duplex with Master Henry, a short-haired mix, curled in the crook of her arm. "Velma just took in a litter of pups with no momma. She needs them cleaned and fed, shots, the whole works."

I tried to wrap my mind around taking on this emergency on top of my current chaos. "Isn't there another volunteer who can help?"

She frowned and reached out to check my forehead with her hand. "Are you sick?"

"Not at all." At her crestfallen look, I started to backtrack but stopped myself. Everyone relied on me to fix things. I usually didn't care. But right now? I couldn't fix a cup of tea, much less my own situation. How could I keep doing things for everyone else? "I'm sorry, I need to study, and I have the night shift at the morgue."

"That's not until seven and you can study there."

A tiny knot of frustration twisted my stomach. "Helping Paws has twenty volunteers. Several others are vet techs and are qualified to do all of that, just like me. Surely one of them is free this afternoon."

She checked my forehead again and made a tutting sound. "You're not running a fever."

Although I attempted patience, my words came out clipped. "Because I'm not sick. I just need time to myself."

I immediately felt guilty when consternation creased her forehead. "Chloe, they're puppies. You love puppies."

Of course, I do. Doesn't everyone? "It's not that, I'm just..." *Busy*, I wanted to finish, but stopped when I thought about spending the next few hours holed up in my room waiting for whoever this "watcher" was to show up. The thought made me fidget. I had an uncomfortable feeling I might already know. "Fine, I'll give her two hours, then I have to study."

Vera smiled and patted my cheek. "I'll tell her you're on your way."

THE PUPPIES WERE the cutest things I'd seen in days.

Only seven weeks old, they needed a lot of attention. I administered their first round of vaccinations and helped clean them up. Like her sister, Velma was generously sized and the puppies loved cuddling on her ample bust. "What breed do you think they are?" she asked. "The Good Samaritan who found them didn't know."

They were fat, furry butterballs at this stage, and I held one up to stare into his face. "Could be long-haired Chihuahuas, but the ears are wrong. Papillon, maybe?"

Velma's eyes lit. "They'll go like hotcakes. We won't have any trouble finding them homes."

The runt of the bunch, a tiny white female, barely able to control her miniature legs, wobbled over and peed on my shoe while I examined a sibling. "Thanks a lot." I handed her brother to Velma, kicking off the soiled shoe. Using a wad of paper towels, I cleaned it as best as I could, realizing I'd just ruined my last decent pair. Well, *I* hadn't. These were my favorites, too, but would now join the others only fit to wear to the morgue.

I heard a funny noise and glanced down. The puppy had sunk her teeth into the hem of my pant leg and was growling and shaking her head back and forth.

"She's feisty." Velma chuckled. She noted her puppy's weight on the intake form. "We need to name them. It's Halloween; that can be our theme."

Themes were big with Velma and her sister. Unnamed litters and bonded pairs often got christened with matching monikers, like Tulip and Rose, Salt and Pepper, Luke and Leia.

"No naming a puppy Jack-o'-lantern," I teased. The white fluffball tugged on my pants again, ferocious in the pursuit of her prey.

"Jack!" Miss Velma held up her dog and looked him in the eyes. "You like it?" The puppy wagged his tail and tried to bite her nose. She pointed at my tiny tyrant. "That one can be Ghost, since she's all white."

The others were quickly named—Pumpkin, Candy, Shadow, and Spooky. I removed Ghost's miniature teeth from my poor clothing and put my shoe back on. "Ready for microchips?"

One of the things I insisted on, as part of the team, is tagging all animals when they come in. It had already saved several runaways.

Velma dug out her bag with the handheld implant "gun" used to insert a tiny chip under the skin between a dog's shoulder blades. Most don't even notice, but a few don't like being restrained and resisted by yelping. You'd think we were torturing them. The information on the chip was registered and allowed a lost pet to be reunited with its owner when the dog was scanned at a vet clinic or shelter.

As she secured the wiggling bodies one at a time, showering them with baby talk, I went to work. Two complained, but the rest were too busy licking Velma's face and accepting treats from her to care.

Ghost was last and had once more attached herself to my pant leg. I wrestled her off it, and lifted her so we were nose to nose. Velma had already begun entering their names and details into her spreadsheet. "You sure act tough for such a little squirt. What did I ever do to you?"

Suddenly, her irises turned orange. She drew back her lips and bared her teeth, snarling. Right before my eyes, the two pound, squirming fluffball broke my hold and morphed into a giant beast.

I gasped and backpedaled, no longer able to hold her. Her canines were the size of spikes, gnashing at the air before her feet hit the floor. She leaped for me, paws the size of baseball mitts, hitting my chest and knocking me to the ground.

TEN

Back hitting the floor, I let out an "oof." The weight of the dog pressed any remaining air from my lungs, her massive head hanging over me. Her glowing eyes stared into mine and drool dripped from her bared lips.

I struggled not to scream. Blinked my eyes, trying to clear the hallucination.

But it was no delusion. Nothing changed as she panted in my face.

Stay calm. A dog is a dog, right? *Show no fear. Assert who's master.* "Nice puppy," I soothed, trying that route first.

She lowered her muzzle, nose sniffing. I instinctively turned my head to avoid drool landing in my mouth.

"There," Velma said, computer keys clicking. "They're all logged in the database. Now we need photos for the social media pages."

Her back was to us and I frantically searched for an idea of how to protect her and the other puppies. Then it hit me —*psychopomp*. They're some type of dog, right? Or are they birds? None of my classes, or vet training, had prepped me for this.

Either way, the one breathing hot puppy breath on me didn't seem friendly, and I wondered if Soul Management Group had rescinded its offer. "Please, no." My voice sounded shaky. "Don't kill me."

A wet tongue licked my cheek.

"Eww," I complained, heart thudding.

Velma seemed completely oblivious. She shifted in her chair, and the others barked and tumbled over each other in the baby playpen next to her desk. When she glanced at me, her face broke into a huge smile. "Aww. That's adorable. I think Ghost has found her new mommy."

"What?" I swiveled my head and looked at the monster dog.

She wasn't a giant anymore. Normal sized again, she peered at me with a humorous, knowing look on her face and pounced up and down on my chest.

A huge sigh of relief bubbled out of me. Had I hallucinated all of that? Maybe the guru's supplements had an extended-release affect.

She lunged forward and bit my nose.

"Ow!" I set her aside and sat up. "Bad dog."

She wagged her tail so hard, she rolled over and over on the floor. Velma laughed. "You have such a way with animals, Chloe."

As I returned Ghost to her siblings, I would swear the dog grinned.

AFTER THE PHOTOSHOOT was over and I was convinced Ghost wasn't a devil dog, regardless of the Hulking-out episode, I agreed to take her home and foster her. Believe me, it was not from the goodness of my heart, as Velma claimed. It was simply because I was petrified she might hurt someone if she morphed into that beast thing again.

Arriving at the duplex, Vera fawned all over her, the cats not so much. They hissed and scattered as Ghost wagged her tail and barked at each of them, happy to establish her alpha-dog status.

All the way home I had continued to ask myself if I had imagined what happened. There were all kinds of freaky things going on, but that didn't mean they were real.

Upstairs in my apartment, I unpacked the foster kit Velma had supplied, complete with a starter bag of food, puppy pads, and a soft bed. After a meal and some roughhousing with a stuffed gerbil bigger than she was, Ghost climbed onto my lap while I did an internet search on grim reapers. She promptly fell asleep.

Gingerly, I placed her in the soft dog bed, but she woke up shortly and returned, scratching at my leg and whimpering until I put her in my lap once more. She circled twice, flopped down, and was snoring in under thirty seconds.

I returned to my search, a gazillion hits coming up for reapers. Narrowing the keywords, I focused on legends and historical stories that traced through nearly all cultures since man had roamed around in tribes. I guess that's when human beings started trying to make sense of life and death.

That rabbit hole led to more and more articles, photos, and religious texts. Hours later, I dragged myself away from the computer for fresh air. I'd missed several messages from Nita again, and one from Aunt Camille, so I responded to both, acting as normal as possible.

My Baby Bomb was long gone, so I grabbed a soda for a

healthy dose of sugar and caffeine. Ghost attacked the gerbil with gusto, her energy restored, and soon, there was white stuffing everywhere. "Great, you're destructive, too." I cleaned up the mess and she wagged, as if asking what was next.

After a trip to the yard, and a sniffing/peeing expedition, I covertly confiscated several cat toys from Vera's stash, and the dog and I returned to my desk. "Okay," I told her, "let's look up psychopomp."

During my previous search, several postings had mentioned that grims themselves often acted as one, taking souls to the afterlife once they were harvested. I read account after account of how and why there were psychopomps and what they did. The logistics of that, and me acting as one, seemed impossible since I was still alive and in a physical body.

"Maybe that's why I need you," I told Ghost. She gnawed on a ball scented with catnip. As I watched, she looked up and barked, giving her opinion. "I can't imagine anyone going with you willingly if you go all demon dog on them. The cute puppy mode, maybe—you're hard to resist like this." I motioned at her current form and she play-growled. I laughed at her tough act. "Yeah, well, don't get too comfortable," I told her. "This is all a misunderstanding. I can't...*harvest* people."

She growled more seriously, and at the same time, the scythe fell off the shelf where I'd laid it. It glowed a sickly green.

I jumped from my chair and backed away. My phone alarm went off, breaking the tension, and I glanced at the screen. Night was falling and it was nearly time for my shift at the morgue. "Hold that thought," I told the weapon, which promptly lost the green glow.

I fed the puppy once more, then stuffed her and the freaky weapon into a duffel bag. The last thing I needed was for it to come to life and scare my landlady.

The robes got stuffed into my dad's old trunk in my closet, and I snagged the cat toys and puppy pads. "You're next." I tucked the wiggling puppy into the bag as well, and she stuck her head out of a small hole I left open on top.

It was the best I could do for now. I hefted the strap over my head and went to work.

ELEVEN

"Behave yourself, beast," I warned as I swiped the keycard at the entrance to the morgue.

The smell was always the first thing to hit—a combo of antiseptic, cleaning products, and a sickly floral air freshener that the night attendant, Mary Lynn, insisted masks the other odors.

The night security guard, Dwayne, barely looked up from his phone. "How ya doing, Chloe?"

"Fantastic. You?"

The morgue was situated in a separate annex from the small hospital and had an underground walkway between. It was only a couple hundred yards from the rear of the police station and the two were connected by a sidewalk. On any given shift, hospital personnel, as well as cops, might visit or drop off bodies.

Dwayne skimmed my bag, his fleshy jowls breaking into a smile. "You got a dog?"

Ghost, eyes bright and ears perked, peeked at him and started clamoring to get out. I freed her before she tumbled to the floor. "She's a foster. She's only seven weeks and can't be left alone yet. She won't be any trouble."

If he saw through that highly probable lie, he didn't act like it.

"Sweet heaven! You got a dog!" The voice was high-pitched and excited, filled with Southern sweetness. Mary Lynn rushed out of the double doors behind Dwayne and snatched Ghost from my arms. Dwayne and I watched the wagging dog lick her face, and then she reciprocated the greeting with the gusto usually reserved for returning soldiers. "She's so sweet!"

This could work to my advantage. "She's available for adoption." Hopefully, she wouldn't morph into a monster again.

As if the dog read my thoughts, she glanced back at me and lifted one edge of her upper lip, showing her incisor.

Okay then.

"I don't think dogs are allowed in here," Dwayne said, lumbering to this feet with a frown. He scratched his head. "I better check."

Barb DeVey was the administrator, and gossip around the place suggested she was right up there with Cruella de Vil when it came to not liking dogs. Mary Lynn and I both responded with a quick, "No!"

While I mentally scrambled for an excuse, my cohort gave the startled guard a charming smile. "She's just a tiny thing, she won't hurt anyone." Mary Lynn's deep brown eyes and black cornrows were accented by a single dimple when she smiled. "We need a little life in the place once in a while, Big D, don'tcha think?"

Dwayne blinked, clearly mesmerized by her pretty charm. "I... Uh..."

"It's only for tonight," I assured him, although I

suspected by the rapt look on his face he didn't hear me. He was absorbed in his fantasy world at the moment, and Mary Lynn was the lead.

Winking, she relinquished the puppy to me and muttered, "Take her on back while Dwayne and I work this out, will you?"

Never look a gift horse, or a morgue attendant, in the mouth is my philosophy. Bag and dog in hand, I used my butt to push through the swinging doors and hustled for the office.

My uncle's commandments were hung on the wall near the sliding doors of the autopsy room.

We speak for the dead. Respect and honor them.

Stick to the facts, and do not suppose you know what their life was like.

In the end, we are all the same—

none of us gets out of this world alive.

Two bodies lay on tables as I passed the windowed autopsy room that we nicknamed The Pit. Two was a lot for Dante's Grove, so it looked to be a busy night. Not ideal for me attempting to hide the dog.

The phone was ringing when I entered the office, the space barely more than a broom closet. Answering it with, "Dante's Grove Morgue," I shifted the handset to a shoulder grip and shoved the bag with the carefully wrapped blade under the desk.

The dull yellow cord was long and floppy after years of use. The minute I set the puppy on the floor, she tangled herself in it. Mock snarling and rolling ensued as a tech at the hospital asked for a report. "I sent the request in yesterday," Randy said grumpily, then brightened. "Do I need to walk over there and get it? I could bring you coffee."

Hard pass. Randy Jarvis was under the mistaken belief I

should go out with him. "No need. I'm emailing it right now."

I disconnected before he could reply, untangled the dog, and woke up the sleeping dinosaur of a computer. There were manila files with sticky notes stacked on the desktop, half-hiding the calendar blotter from 1994. That's when the last renovation had been done here and the hospital put us out of mind.

I logged into our internal network and located the request. Ghost wandered the office, tiny as it was, sniffing and taste testing anything she could put her tongue on.

"Don't do that," I told her as I searched for the former patient's autopsy report. 'Dinosaur' might've been a compliment when it came to the computer. 'Snail' was more like it, the autopsy files many layers deep in the shared network. The hard drive hummed and whirled, every click of the mouse producing another long wait.

The crash of the lost and found box alerted me that the puppy had managed to climb on a low shelf in the corner, spilling the contents to the floor. She pounced on a knit cap, and it didn't put up a fight. Her tiny teeth ripped the yarn to pieces before I could send off the report.

"Isn't she precious?" Mary Lynn stood in the doorway. She scooped her up and Ghost nipped her nose. She laughed. "I could just eat you up."

Or be eaten by her. "Two autopsies tonight?"

She tucked Ghost under her arm, scratching the puppy's chest. "Found together in the park. Weird, right? No obvious COD."

An alarm went off in my head. "Last night?" I asked hesitantly.

She nodded. "Your uncle has his work cut out on this one."

The outer doors flapped and Ghost growled at the noise. Mary Lynn looked over her shoulder, and I rose slightly out of my seat to peek through the window, afraid Randy or another staff member might be visiting. I couldn't take the chance they'd give up Ghost's presence to the hospital administrator.

There was no one there though, and Mary Lynn wiggled her fingers. "Ghosts," she teased with a wink. She liked to claim the spirits of the dead hung around until we were done with them. "Anyway, I better prep before Morty gets here."

I shivered at the thought she might be right. Reluctantly, she turned the dog over to me. Ghost licked my face, then jumped down to attack a lone shoe from the box.

My uncle arrived in a whirlwind of aftershave and cannoli an hour later. Dressed in smart slacks and a button-down, he'd slicked back his midnight black hair and shaved the stubble that he could never quite seem to tame. Ghost was sleeping by that point, having worn herself out and I put a finger to my lips when he entered the cramped space to offer the container of my favorite dessert to me. "Did you finally cave?" he teased, kissing my cheek. "I knew you would."

Ghost snored and I glanced at her. "She's a foster."

He winked at me. "Right. Don't let Barbie see her."

Once he'd donned his scrubs, he and Mary Lynn finally started on the couple in the other room. I lowered the blinds on the single window, and rubbed my eyes. In between wrangling the puppy, all I'd managed to accomplish so far was filling out two requests—one from the hospital and another from Detective Adams at the police station.

Hoping for a few minutes to study before Uncle Morty handed me the paperwork and dictation for tonight's work,

I sank in the chair, flinching at the shrill squeak it emitted, and pulled out my textbook.

Growing up with veterinarians as parents, I knew more about animals than I did humans. The words in the book blurred together and I wondered why I bothered to study. I could run circles around Nita and the other vet students, simply from the knowledge and experiences I already had.

But tests had to be taken, and professors preferred regurgitating the material from their lectures, rather than real life. I had a decent memory, and recall of written details was strong, so I kept at it, studying the lessons and reciting them week after week. Whatever it took to graduate and become a full-fledged vet. I needed to make my mom and dad proud.

Opening the textbook, I started reading.

TWELVE

An hour later, I was half-asleep, the words about feline lungs and hearts blurring on the page. I felt a cool breeze on my face, and the scent of warm caramel and old libraries replaced the chemical odor.

Miraculously, the dog was still out, her soft snores and twitching legs bringing a smile to my face. Yawning, I stood and stretched, wondering about the pleasant scent invading the office, but not seeing any reason for it. Had Mary Lynn brought in a new air freshener?

My blood tingled. Maybe I was just hungry. I grabbed a dollar from the wallet tucked in the bag to hit the vending machines.

Classic rock blaring from his speaker system, Uncle Morty was finishing up the first autopsy—the woman—and didn't glance up as I passed. While he sewed up the chest, Mary Lynn cleaned their tools, giving me a quick wave and a smile from behind her face mask.

The night was cloudy and a light mist was falling, but I preferred taking the outside sidewalk to the hospital, rather than the underground tunnel. The night staff was sparse, the cafeteria closed. The line of vending machines was substantial, though, and one can of soda and an egg sandwich later, I trudged back, rubbing my eyes and hoping the shot of caffeine would get me through the midnight hours.

My uncle and Mary Lynn were on a break at that point, The Pit eerily quiet. Entering the office as noiselessly as I could and praying Ghost still slumbered, I came to an abrupt halt. Not only was she awake, she appeared to be hovering above the worn seat of the guest chair in the corner. Her miniature tail wagged furiously, front paws braced against something invisible as her tongue licked the air.

"What the...?"

"Don't be alarmed," a familiar voice said.

My blood tingled even more, an all-out race taking place up and down my insides. Before my incredulous eyes, Killion became visible. Dressed in a dark suit, he patiently endured the puppy's adoration.

My heart attack was brief, and I hurriedly shut the door, double-checking that no one was around. "What are you doing here, and how did you do that?"

Ignoring my questions, he stood, setting the wriggling dog on the desk. "Where are the robes?"

He was taller than I remembered, but I'd been distracted that night. I was close to five-seven and he topped that by five to six inches. The tingling inside me ratcheted up a notch and I caught myself breathing a little deeper to inhale his calming scent and wondering how my hair looked.

Stop it. My libido is starved for attention, that's all it is, I assured myself. Setting down the soda and half-eaten snack, I ignored the reaction and forced my face into what I hoped was a neutral expression. As soon as my hands were free,

Ghost jumped into my arms, nearly knocking me sideways. Such a tiny dog, but so strong. "Are you here to take them back?" My voice sounded a bit too hopeful. "I don't have them with me, but I can get them after my shift."

"Rookies," he muttered and my hackles went up. Good looking or not, he was already getting on my nerves. He brushed dog hair from his vest and pants—that suit had to cost more than my semester tuition. "You have a job now. Your robes should be accessible at all times."

"I *do* have a job." Ghost wiggled, reaching for him and I set her on the floor. She reared up on her hind feet and danced before scratching at his pant leg. Traitor. "Two, in fact, and they don't like it if I show up in depressing costumes."

He pinched the bridge of his nose, ignoring the puppy. "And the scythe?"

I pointed. "Under the desk."

"That will have to do." He eyed Ghost, still begging for his attention. "Bring the dog as well."

He reached for the doorknob and I launched myself forward to put a hand out and stop it from opening. "Just a minute." I slammed it shut once more. "I need answers, starting with, are *you* my watcher?"

"Watcher is an antiquated term. I prefer mentor." That uncanny stillness came over him, the violet eyes going dark and hard. "And yes. Temporarily."

He was not happy about it. Made two of us. "What does that mean—temporarily?"

"I am a detective, not a watcher. However, due to the circumstances, SMG has asked me to step in and assist you, since we have a...relationship."

That was pushing it. "Detective? Like a police officer?"

Ghost sat at his feet staring up with fangirl puppy eyes.

He removed his hand from the knob and buttoned his blazer. "The grim you exterminated is part of a much larger rogue group, as I mentioned. SMG retained my services to uncover how large and who is heading it."

"So what exactly are you? I mean, in the supernatural department."

"Not your concern." He glanced at his watch. "We must go. Get the scythe. Time is running out."

A chill washed over my skin. "For who?"

"Whom," he corrected. "Bring the dog."

The Pit was still empty as we passed. The bag on my shoulder felt heavier than when I'd arrived. Ghost wiggled in my arms, excited, but all I felt was dread. I wondered if she knew what was about to happen. "I have a moral dilemma," I said.

Dwayne was at the station. "Don't we all?"

That's when I realized he didn't see Killion, who was right behind me. I continued walking. "Just taking the dog out. I'll be back soon."

His attention returned to the game he played on his phone, and he grunted his confirmation.

The night sky greeted us and Ghost nearly catapulted from my arms. Puppies this young weren't supposed to touch the ground, since they haven't had all their shots yet, but I had the distinct impression nothing could hurt her.

"How do you do that?" I asked Killion. "Keep people from seeing you?"

He watched Ghost sniff around. "That man has a dull mind and wouldn't believe in the supernatural if he was struck upside the head with it. A mere suggestion to ignore me was all I needed."

"Don't insult my friends. And previously, you were invisible to me."

"When you initially walked in, you weren't expecting anyone to be there. It took a few seconds for your inner eye to register my presence, that's all. You can see me because we are connected, whether I use glamour or not."

Honestly, I should have been freaked out about it, but I was kind of hoping it was a cool new trick he'd be able to teach me.

Ghost relieved herself and bounded after us as Killion led the way toward the rear entrance of the hospital. "I won't kill anyone," I told him firmly. "I've given it a lot of thought. You're going to have to find someone else."

His footsteps never faltered. "Not an option."

The doors of the entrance slid open at our approach. I picked up Ghost, hoping I wouldn't get in trouble for flaunting the no pet rule clearly posted next to the firearms ban.

Uncle Morty was exiting just then with a tray from the cafeteria in hand. "Don't tell your aunt," he said dipping his chin at the assortment of plastic-wrapped items he carried. "I need the extra calories tonight."

His generous belly said differently, but I saluted him in silent unity. My aunt was constantly putting him on a diet, and was rather rigid about what she allowed him to consume. Tricky, since she created confections no one in their right mind could ignore.

"You can't bring dogs in, you know," he called over his shoulder. He appeared unaware of my companion. "Only service or therapy canines are allowed."

"I'm training her for therapy." The lie rolled off my tongue with ease and I instantly felt guilty for it.

The doors swished shut, Uncle Morty giving me a wink as he continued on his way. Unity again between us.

"The psychopomp *is* a therapy dog of sorts," Killion

stated. The antiseptic smell here was weaker. "They shift into a welcoming companion at times to assist souls into the afterlife."

"Oh, I've seen her do that." We passed the receptionist's desk. The night attendant here was playing a computer game behind the raised counter and barely acknowledged us. "Believe me, no one's going to want to cross to the afterlife with that beast breathing down their neck. Ghost might chase them there, but she's not suitable, nor friendly, as a psychopomp."

He tapped the elevator button and glanced around. We were alone, the distant sound of a nurse paging an orderly over the speaker system. "If it makes it any easier, you're not killing anyone."

I blew out a long, slow breath. "That's a relief." I stepped inside when the doors opened and he pushed the button marked three. "What *am* I doing? I thought that's what grims did—harvest souls."

He crossed his hands in front of him and stared at the panel. "This particular soul is a half-mag."

"Mag—I don't understand that term."

"Magical. Those without magic are often referred to as no-mages or mundanes."

"Like in Harry Potter."

An eyebrow twitched. "This creature has no control over his abilities, but still uses them to create havoc in the mundane world. He was scheduled to die as a result of his last robbery, but ended up in a coma instead. Brain dead and living on borrowed time, his ghost haunts the hospital, continuing to cause chaos."

Sounded like it fit with all the other wackadoodle stuff going on around me. "How exactly do I, um, reap him?"

His handsome reflection in the mirrored door showed restrained patience. "With your clever wit."

It took me a moment to process that. "Did you just make a joke?"

His face remained immobile. "You have the scythe and a psychopomp. Are you truly that dense?"

Irritation bubbled under my skin. "I don't typically walk around waving a big blade at people or sic'ing a dog on a comatose patient."

The elevator dinged softly. "You'll never rise above GR second class if you can't figure some of this out on your own."

"GR what?"

The elevator slid to a stop and the doors opened. We stepped out. "You're starting at the bottom of the ladder, of course."

Of course.

Here was chaos. The nurses' station was busy, patient alerts sounding, phones ringing, and two different aides running up and down the corridors. An attendant was on a phone at a computer station. "I told you, it's just gone," he stated sharply. "The whole program disappeared."

The lights overhead flickered and a shadowy figure laughed as it whizzed by us.

"Grim 281, meet Talon Harris." Killion patted me on the back, shoving me in the direction of the ghost. "Go get him."

THIRTEEN

y palm tingled; my tattoo warmed. I had no idea what I was doing, but I was determined to get it over with.

"Hey," I yelled at the ghost. The nurses' station was in such commotion, no one looked my way.

Talon Harris did. He pulled up in mid-air, did a double-take when he realized I was staring at him, and raced back to me. "You can see me?"

A breeze of cool air wafted over me. "Quit being a jerk and meet me in your room."

Marching down the hall, no idea where I was going, I was nevertheless on a mission. Killion grabbed my arm, pivoting me toward the opposite direction. "Room 303."

"Right. I knew that."

"You can't have a dog in here," a nurse's aide called as I strode past the desk.

I didn't even look at her and kept going. "Therapy dog," I replied.

Killion fell into step beside me. "What's your plan?"

Plan? Ha! "I'm kinda new to this, in case you haven't figured it out. Is our ghost following?"

"No, hence the suggestion you develop a plan on how to handle the situation."

Life must be easy for Mr. Type A. "Forgive me, Your Royal Pain in the Backside." I hesitated outside the door. "You threw me into this with no training or guidance, so don't lecture me about a plan, or the lack thereof."

He may have been annoying, but like a gentleman, he held the door open for me. "Pull out the scythe, get him near it, and let it do its thing."

Ghost barked, as if in agreement.

Sounded simple enough. "Do I have to swing it at him?"

The room was quiet, except for the ventilator and heart monitor. The shades were drawn. Talon's body lay immobile, a wad of white bandages around his skull. His chest rose and fell mechanically.

"Hopefully not, if your ability to use it last night is any indication of skill."

I couldn't tell if he was teasing or not, but there was a trace of ridicule in his voice. As we neared the bed, Ghost leaped from my arms and landed on Talon's stomach. His belly depressed, but barely emitted any response beyond that.

"The snarky comments aren't helpful," I stated.

"My bad."

Studying his face, I could see he was unapologetic, but at least he was here, giving me support. What little of it he had offered, anyway. Still, it was better than doing this totally alone.

He caught my eyes. "Sincerely. I apologize for my lack of manners. I wasn't expecting to mentor a new grim."

"Imagine my surprise at becoming one."

Those intense eyes turned dark and bored into me. "You're actually doing better than—"

Talon's ghost materialized between us and sneered. "What do you want?"

I opened the gym bag and drew out the scythe. The tattoo burned. "For you to go to the afterlife where you belong."

He glanced at the weapon and laughed.

FOURTEEN

His ghost flew under the bed, came up and rose over my head, and then vanished out the door—going right through it.

"Well done, rookie," Killion said.

I heard the smirk in his voice, even if his face was devoid of emotion. "Excuse me? Like you could have done better. You said to get this thing"—I shook the blade—"near him and *let it do its thing.*"

Ghost jumped up and down on the man's stomach, wagging her tail as if enjoying our bickering.

The lights in the room flickered, someone screamed in the corridor, and I shoved the scythe back inside the bag. Regardless of not having a plan, I was still fired up enough not to care that things were going sideways. Talon was my first job and although I didn't relish what I had to do, my competitive streak kicked in hard. The ghost was not going to get the best of me, and neither was my "watcher." If I had to endure another rude comment from the peanut gallery, I was going to take a swing at him, too. "Come on," I said to the dog, scooping her off the bed.

I marched out the door, hearing the call buttons buzzing and nurses and aides yelling. Tension zinged in the air as their screeches and bellows echoed in the hallway. Whether or not Killion followed, I didn't care.

Talon emerged from a patient's room and entered its companion across the way. Another beep was added to the cacophony.

Neither the sick, nor their caregivers, were having a peaceful night, and it was time I put a stop to this ghost's obnoxiousness. Striding across the linoleum, I felt a rush of confidence, purpose. My hand warmed and the bag trembled, as if the scythe was actively trying to get into my grip.

Without knocking, I slipped in. An elderly woman with gray hair lay wide-eyed in bed with a sheet drawn up to her chin. "What's happening out there?"

Talon played with her remote. He couldn't seize it, but a crackling energy bolted from his fingertips, causing it to activate the TV in the upper corner. Scads of late night talk shows, sitcom reruns, and shopping channels flipped by at a schizophrenic pace. The woman flinched and hunkered farther down.

"Don't worry," I reassured her. "It's just a malfunction of the power hub down the street. Nothing will hurt you. It'll be fixed shortly."

Talon barely acknowledged my presence, too busy juicing the remote.

"What a precious dog." The woman's attention locked on Ghost. "What's her name?"

My psychopomp surged forward, scrambling to get to her. I half-stumbled trying not to drop her. "Petunia," I lied.

The door swung open and Killion entered, filling the room with his presence. That got Talon's attention, and he stopped zapping and prepared to dart out.

"Touch the wall," the vampire growled.

I didn't know if he was speaking to me or to the ghost. As the woman made over Ghost, oblivious to the two men, I reached out and did what he said. He blocked the door and also placed his palm on the dingy wall next to him. A silver light ran around the edges of the room, tickling my hand with a low energy buzz.

That's when I realized Killion looked different, predatory. His features were the same, but his eyes had changed. The darkest espresso once more, there was an icy violet ring around his pupils.

The itching in my other hand became painful. Talon raced for the wall connecting this room to the next. He didn't get far and bounced off. Trapped.

"What are you doing?" he cried and slammed his body against the wall. The light flared and knocked him backwards.

Struggling to unzip the bag, the scythe banging around inside, I had to take a deep breath and focus. Killion's energy was flooding my system and I had the odd sensation the blood he'd shared with me was responding to it. Maybe that was why everything in me tingled when he was near. That was a slight relief, putting my libido theory to rest.

My hearing sharpened, as did my vision. I could make out the distinctive smells of the dog, the bed linens, the patient herself. Even the IV drip in her vein had an odor that tickled my nostrils.

The moment the zipper gave, the weapon flew into my palm. Talon, still bouncing around off the walls and swearing at us, whizzed past my head, then stopped and frowned. "Pink daisies?"

Confused, I glanced at the blade. I saw the cold steel

and wooden handle, glowing with a similar light that infused the walls of the room.

Talon hovered closer. "Those were my mom's favorite. How did you know?"

The scythe, like the dog earlier, acted as if it would bolt from my grip. The same sensation I'd had the previous night took over and something otherworldly seemed to raise the weapon and ready it to swing. I had to think fast. Words tumbled from my mouth. "She sent them." I nodded, warming to my own story. "She wanted to let you know it's safe for you to...cross over...to the afterlife. She's waiting for you."

His eyes met mine. "She is?"

There was so much longing, so much grief in those two words. So much hope. I felt the sudden truth of it and nodded again. Maybe all of those medium shows Nita had made me watch were paying off. My mouth opened and I began talking once more, not knowing where the words came from. "The world hasn't been easy for you, has it, since she passed? She knows how hard you've struggled. It's time to release all of that and rest. She can't wait to see you again, Talon."

His eyes took on a glazed expression, focused on the scythe and mesmerized by the flowers he saw.

"I miss food," he told me. From the extra thirty pounds he carried around his middle, I assumed he must have enjoyed it. Couldn't blame him. I hadn't really thought about it before, but eating was an enormous pleasure that spirits couldn't savor. "I went to the cafeteria just to smell it."

The woman on the bed laughed at Ghost and the dog licked her wrinkled cheek. Somehow the magic in this room kept her oblivious and I was grateful. I glanced at Killion, and realized he was probably the one creating this...what had he called it? A glamour?

The scythe handle grew hotter in my fingers. "I'm sorry," I told Talon. "I don't know about food in the afterlife, but I hear there are lots of other perks."

His bottom lip trembled. "Can you put me back in my body?"

Once more, I glanced at my mentor. He shook his head. "I'm afraid that's not my area," I told the ghost, "and I wouldn't be here if that were an option."

The flowers continued to draw him in and he took a step closer. "I miss her."

"I bet she was a good mom."

His eyes shone with tears. "Always believed in me. I let her down."

"That's in the past, and she was always proud of you." *Touch the flowers.* "She loves you and wants to see you again."

He reached out and I held my breath. "I want to see her, too." His fingers floated centimeters from the blade. "Does it hurt? When you...you know?"

Killion again shook his head, this time in confirmation.

"No," I told Talon.

A snore suddenly echoed from the bed. Ghost had put the patient to sleep. As the ghost touched the scythe disguised as flowers, two things happened at once—the weapon swung and Ghost morphed.

Not into her devil dog appearance, but into a kindly looking woman who had Talon's nose. "Hello, sweetie," she said to him. "Let's go home."

The psychopomp and ghost disappeared.

FIFTEEN

The rush from his spirit leaving took me by surprise. All feeling fled my legs, my strength going with it. Unable to control my limbs, I fell against the wall and slid to the floor. My vision whited out, my breath catching in my throat.

Killion called my name, but it was a distant buzz. The distinctive code red alarm went off on the floor, adding another layer of background drone, all of it dimmed by the gushing waterfall inside my head.

The sensation was exhilarating and blissful, the best drug ever. I rode the high and sensed, as any junkie would, that I never wanted to come down. Much like that moment right before you drop into sleep, it beckoned me as a lover to let go. Give in. Succumb.

A tiny voice urged me not to. *Fight it*, it demanded. *It's not your time. You have work to do.*

That sounded like my mother. My conditioned response was to do what she said, even if she was dead, but overwhelming desire to let go of those thoughts, to snuff out her voice of reason, filled me. I was connected to something much, much bigger. Deeper. The omniscient sense of power and peace was impossible to ignore.

Even blinded, I could see everything on a screen inside my lids. Sense all that existed. I was connected to all beings. The static-y vacuum in my head became the voice of angels.

My mother cut through the choir once more. "Chloe, *wake up.* Now!"

"Mom?"

Through the glistening whiteness, the outline of her form emerged. She appeared to vibrate, the air around her resembling heatwaves rising from pavement on a hot, summer day. Her face became more lucid, a gentle smile on it. My heart broke. "I'm always with you, and your father and I are waiting for you on the other side when it's time. All is well."

She faded away and I reached for her. "No, wait! Mom, come back."

A sharp pain in my arm assailed me. The fiery sensation burned along my veins, jerking me out of the dream.

Thanks to the rabid dog now standing on my chest, that was no longer an option. My connection to the other side broken, my vision cleared. The cold reality of life slapped me upside the head, the sounds of the hospital rushing back.

I wasn't on the floor anymore. I was laying in a hospital bed with Ghost's scary face staring down at mine. Drool dripped from her fangs. At the same time, she wagged her tail.

"Oh, get off," I groaned.

"Good, you're back." Killion stood at my side. "You have to learn to control yourself."

The psychopomp morphed into her puppy version and licked my nose. "What just happened?"

"Soul transference." He helped me sit up, catching me

when the room spun and I nearly toppled over. "Yours will most often experience what the retrieved soul does as it crosses to the afterlife. It's considered a job perk by some."

I blinked my eyes and rubbed my temples. "I saw my mom." I wiped drool from my cheek, hoping it was Ghost's and not mine. "I didn't want to return."

Killion made sure I was steady on the edge of the mattress. "Hence, the need for control."

"How do I do that?" More importantly, why did I want to? "It was nirvana, heaven, utopia. Wait—*was* it heaven?"

"Come," he said, ignoring the question. He grabbed my bag and headed for the door. "We have more to accomplish."

"Why wasn't my dad there?" The room slipped and heaved when I stood, and I had to grip the rail to steady myself. "Can I talk to my mom whenever I want? Wait!"

The door stood open, my mentor gone.

I swore, blinked until my vision cleared and I felt steady enough to walk, then followed.

The hallways were quieter now. As Ghost pranced after Killion, I forced my shaky legs to work. When we reached the elevator, I picked up the dog and cradled her, the blissed out feeling a soft glow in my chest.

Mom was in some form of a heavenly afterlife. I was sure of it.

I was also sure that, given the chance, I would go there again in a heartbeat.

SIXTEEN

In the elevator, Killion offered a few answers. "The afterlife is different for each soul. Your version will be distinct from mine. I am not a grim and have not experienced what you just did, so my knowledge is limited to what other reapers have shared concerning the topic. I do not know why your mother came to you, nor why your father didn't. What I do know is that you must guard against allowing transference to happen before your soul contract is up. You could upset the balance of things if you cross early."

Ghost was sated, dozing in my arms. I feared if I closed my eyes, even for a moment, I'd drift off to sleep, too. "I'm a bit fuzzy on the whole soul contract thing."

"Each soul is incarnated multiple times. Before you enter a body, your soul agrees on a set of terms provided by SMG regarding where you'll live, who your parents will be, and a host of other details and events. One of those includes when your life will end and by what means."

"Sounds...fatalistic. What about free will?"

"There is a balance." He flicked his gaze my way in the reflective panel of the door. "Not all events and actions are subjugated to fate and destiny. Yet, I have found that much of what we believe is free will, isn't."

Cheery thought. "Was my parents' car crash part of their soul contract?"

The violet eyes caught and held mine this time. "I do not know, and asking such questions is a waste of time. The outcome cannot be altered."

Thinking about fate versus free will was a rabbit hole I didn't have the strength to fall into at the moment. Downstairs, before we reached the exit doors, I noticed another ghost. "Should I harvest that one?" I asked.

A woman entered through the sliding doors and strolled toward us. She was strikingly beautiful with dark hair and eyes, and dressed in a tight skirt with a flippy edge.

"No," Killion replied, his attention snapping to her. "That soul is hers."

Dramatic, full red lips. Cleavage spilling out of a deep V in her sweater. High heels that exaggerated her hip swing like a 1950's bombshell actress. The lips curved when she registered my mentor, and something kicked in my chest. "Killion, darling." She drew out his name in a throaty tone that was smooth as melting butter and had a rich cadence. A *money* cadence, as if she'd grown up surrounded by it.

Kill, that voice said in my head. My palm itched for the handle of the scythe. No heat from the tattoo, though.

Stop that, I mentally reprimanded the blade.

Killion's body appeared relaxed, but I sensed the now familiar field of energy wrapping around us like a protective bubble. "Jacqueline," he responded, acknowledging her with little more than a nod.

The black-as-night gaze flicked between the two of us. Her gaze bore into mine as though she could see inside my head, and I had the sensation of a mosquito buzzing around in my skull.

"New girl?"

Was she talking to him or me? "Sorry," I said, "I don't believe we've met."

Her smile became a smirk as she sashayed past my outstretched hand. "Good luck."

Kill.

I still wasn't sure which of us she spoke to. "Nice meeting you, too," I called after her, scrubbing my tingling palm on my pants. The light in the hall seemed to follow her, as though she were sucking it up as she walked. Her hair gleamed, and I watched over my shoulder until she turned the corner and disappeared. "Who was *that?*"

The bubble faded. "Jacqueline Vermouth, GR 1st Class. She gets the majority of cases in this area. At least, the more palpable, non-magical, ones." Killion tugged on my arm to get me walking again. "I'd advise staying out of her way. She's an elite reaper and doesn't play well with others."

She seemed familiar, but I had no idea why. "Hence the bubble?"

"You felt that?"

"Sure did. Another of your magical skills?"

"You are...odd."

"Thanks. You're rude." I wasn't attracted to women in general, but regardless of her snooty attitude, her beauty was undeniable. I glanced back once more. "She's so..."

"Yes," he agreed, although I hadn't finished the sentence. "She is."

We continued to the exit. "It felt like she was reading my mind."

He seemed unfazed by this revelation. "Probably. She

was a level six psychic before she was recruited to work for SMG."

Level six? "I assume that's powerful?"

He nodded.

"Were you a psychic, too? Is that why you can…"—I made twirling finger motions at my head—"use telepathy on me?"

Outside, the air temp had dropped. "I'm unsure of why you could hear me before we became linked by my blood. Perhaps it is you who are psychic."

"Me?" I laughed, then took a deep inhale, trying to clear my mind as well as my lungs. "By the way, invasion of privacy much? We never did discuss your mind reading."

"Yours and Jacqueline's paths are bound to intersect, but avoid her when possible." Killion slowed, the sky twinkling above us. "I would never invade your privacy, as you can tell by the fact I've stayed out of your head since I discovered your abilities."

Abilities—a kind way of saying I was a freak? I placed Ghost down for a pee break and she scavenged around before relieving herself in a flower bed. "I'm not psychic and I don't have 'abilities.' If I did, I'd use them to ace my classes and mind-meld people into doing what I want." I grinned.

"You're far too nice for that."

I narrowed my eyes. He was right. "You don't know me," I argued.

"I wasn't sure Talon would go that easily." He gazed at the hospital. "You did well for your first time. A natural."

The compliment shouldn't have caused such a reaction, but my cheeks warmed at the praise. I lifted my chin. "First class overachiever, at your service. Why do you think I have no social life? Also, stop redirecting the conversation. It's annoying. Man, am I hungry."

A rare smile tugged at the corner of his lips. "You should eat. It will help your energy. You'll be safe in the morgue. I'll leave you now, but will return when I can."

Be still my heart. "I have more questions."

"We have plenty of time for them. For now, give your notice to both jobs, forget school, and perhaps read the reaper manual you were provided with."

Never in my life did I expect someone to tell me to become the equivalent of a dropout, as well as a delinquent. "Should I rob a bank, too?"

He didn't respond, simply walked off and disappeared into the shadows at the edge of the complex.

"Wait, what manual?" Ghost caught up with me, lifting her front paws to be picked up. I did as she requested, and she made a gurgling noise and belched. "Eww," I complained, barely managing to hold her out as she regurgitated a large clump of grossness.

The blob fell to the grass as she licked her lips and burped again. The stomach contents on the ground had paper in it. I hoisted her up to look her in the eye. "Oh no, you did not."

She wagged and tried to lick my face.

The dog from hell had eaten my reaper homework.

SEVENTEEN

When my shift ended at seven the next morning, Killion was waiting for me.

I'd had so much energy after harvesting Talon, I'd thoroughly cleaned and reorganized the office, and assisted Mary Lynn in doing the same with The Pit. As I left the hospital grounds at a brisk pace, my watcher came into view, leaning against the low stone fence of a Victorian house down the street from the police station. His feet crossed at the ankles, his face full of shadows, he was again in a suit that looked like it had come straight off a NYC runway. The rising sun shone off the damp road, but stopped before breeching the sidewalk where he waited.

Ghost barked a greeting, hanging out of my bag. The tightness in his lips left and he raised a corner of them to smile at the dog, or maybe both of us. Either way, it sent a warm cascade of desire through certain parts of my anatomy.

I pulled up short. *Down girl.* I might be hard up for male attention—and sure, he was drop-dead handsome in that dark, mysterious, supernatural way—but he was also a touch scary and a whole lot annoying. Like, more so than anyone I'd ever met.

The dog and I joined him in the shadows. "You don't have to walk me home," I stated.

He boosted off the stones with predatory grace. "Did you read the manual?"

We began walking, a few damp leaves clinging to the sidewalk. "Yeah, about that. The dog ate it."

He flicked a glance at her. His only rebuke was a strained sigh. The bag jiggled against my hip from her feverishly wagging tail. She had it bad.

"You really brought me back to life in that alley, didn't you?"

Another flick of his gaze, this time at me. The continuing silence filled the air between us, and I took that as confirmation.

After my high had worn off, I'd stewed. Too many questions were floating in my head. I doubted any manual could answer them. "In all seriousness, what if I screw up?"

"I'm here to make sure you don't."

His confidence was reassuring. Sort of. "You're going to haunt my every waking hour in order to guarantee that?"

He didn't so much as shrug. He also didn't seem happy about it. "If necessary."

The thought both excited and frightened me. The excited part worried me more than anything else. "Look, I *save* people and animals. That's my thing. Death is...not."

"How is it you save humans? You are not a medical doctor."

That was easy. "Coffee. Nectar of the gods."

He stopped walking. This time I got a full-on stare.

I pulled up as well and stared back. "I work in a coffee shop. Trust me, I've saved a lot of lives by providing caffeine to folks who might go postal on their friends and family without it."

This garnered a shake of his head. A pigeon landed a few feet away, cooing and pecking at the strip of grass next to the sidewalk. We resumed our pace. "I believe you give the substance too much credit."

I thought about his magic, the blood he'd shared with me. My suspicions as to what he was made me shiver. Yet, it felt weirdly rude to burst out another round of *what are you?* "Do you even drink coffee?"

"On occasion. Not the cheap stuff you sell."

I held back my argument. He stayed in the shadows of the trees that lined the street. Because if he didn't, the sun's rays might incinerate him?

The pigeon was suddenly scooped up and lifted out of our way, deposited farther down on the lawn. I sighed, knowing I had to be rude regardless of how awkward I felt. "What are you?" I asked. "For real."

"Did you resign from your job at the morgue?

"Diversion will not work this time." Or most of the time. Unless there was chocolate involved. "Tell me the truth."

"I will when the time is right."

"Why not now?"

"We are only getting to know each other. Have I asked personal questions of you?"

"Mostly, you've ordered me around." Everything seemed more vibrant this morning, including him. I was alive. That was a win. "I'm not going to like it, am I? The truth about you?"

"You need sleep."

"Actually, like my adoring public, I need caffeine." I veered left, waiting for a morning commuter in a red compact to pass before I jaywalked across. The Bean was only two blocks north.

Killion was next to me before I could blink. "You must eliminate unnecessary trips for now."

I hawked a glance back at where he'd been and gaped at him next to me. "How did you do that? Wait, I forgot. Magic." I cut through a narrow alley between the dry cleaners and an Asian restaurant, both closed at the moment. The pungent odor of peanut oil and dry cleaning fluid assaulted my nostrils. My eyes threatened to water—since when had I become so sensitive to smells and noises? "Are you avoiding the sun?"

He made no effort to confirm or deny it. Nor did he put my theory to rest.

"By the way," I continued, "I think Jaqueline might have been watching you Friday night. There was a woman in the shadows when I passed you at Boozy's."

"I did not sense her. It was most likely my second in command, Simone. She often stays close."

I hadn't really seen her. It had been too dark. "I'm not giving up everything for this reaper gig. A year from now, when my contract is up, I'll still have a life to go back to and bills to pay."

"A year and thirty days, if you survive the probationary period. At that time, there will be plenty of minimum wage vacancies you can fill with your mundane skills."

The way he said it rankled my nerves. I stepped out from the alley and into the sunshine, the faint scent of ground beans already carrying on the air and seducing me like a siren's call. "You're funny," I said.

"I am not attempting humor. It is fact."

The very thought of a triple-shot latte soothed me. "What do you like, if you don't drink coffee? Healthy stuff, like smoothies?" He was extremely buff under his fine threads. "If it's the caffeine you're worried about, my friend, Nita, makes a really delicious chai drink that—"

He grabbed my shoulder, fingers sinking in deep, and stopped me from stepping off the curb. "Grim 281, you need to go home, ward the building, and stay there."

The tension in his voice triggered something deep in my brain, sending a hot wash of primal fight-or-flight instinct racing down my spine. Not this again. "Why?" I glanced around. "What's wrong?" *And how do I ward a building?*

"Your reaction to the harvest of Talon's soul alerted certain entities to your new profession. They know you killed Gustafson and aren't happy."

"The rogues?" Ice set up shop in my blood. "Aren't happy, as in they're going to post rude comments about me on social media?"

Before he could reply, three men, dressed in black from head to toe, emerged from a copse of trees.

Kill, the voice said. This time, my tattoo fired up, making me gasp.

Matching grins on their half-masked faces, the trio flashed their scythes. Then, moving as one, they descended on us.

EIGHTEEN

I screamed, dropped the bag, and ran like the girl I am.

Later, I would tell myself it was a normal reaction considering a grim had recently killed me.

My attempt to flee was cut short by one of Killion's bubbles. The boundary of it was pliable, like running into a balloon, and it stretched around my fleeing body, but slowed my progress. I knew before I came to a full stop that it was going to catapult me back to the scene.

As if in slow motion, I did, indeed, snap back. I registered Ghost had morphed into her psychopomp version, paws braced and teeth bared. Killion had also shapeshifted to an extent, all fangs and claws now.

Still airborne, my hand flew out and the scythe smacked into my palm. From the backward momentum, I somersaulted over myself, crashing into Ghost's side. I dropped to the ground with a jolt, teeth jarring and causing me to bite my tongue. The scythe whacked the concrete.

The three attackers paused their advance, and even with their masks, I could tell they were slightly perplexed. I hoped it was due to my incredible ninja moves and not my landing in a heap at their feet.

"Get up," Killion growled. Like *literally* growled. It was a guttural sound that made the hair on my arms stand up. He'd gone pale, his face distorted. His irises were red.

Amaze-horror aside, I didn't have time to gawk. I tasted blood. Our attackers, seemingly over their surprise, smelled it—they wanted mine.

My palm buzzed, my tattoo flashed white hot. A rush of adrenaline hit my system like I'd downed that coveted triple shot. I jumped to my feet, sneakers squeaking on the frosty sidewalk, and launched myself at them with a loud cry.

Okay, technically, the scythe did the launching. I actually cringed, made a mouse-like noise in the back of my throat, and attempted to bolt once more.

The death blade was having none of it, the handle glued to my palm as it jerked me forward and hacked at the closest predator. *Kill*, it commanded.

Yep, the blade could get in my head, too.

Killion swung away, elongated claws swiping at the chest of his target. Ghost pounced on the third and his scythe, half the size of mine, sliced into her left shoulder. Her paws knocked him back and her massive jaws snapped at his face. He screamed.

My blade seemed to possess a life of its own. It used my body to fend off my attacker, my arms and legs making swift, hard punches and jabs. The distant part of my brain not screaming in terror actually admired my agility and defense moves. It was like I was channeling every movie fight scene I'd ever watched.

Killion got the upper hand with his grim, but Ghost was bleeding. Even with her size, the man she fought was inflicting more damage on her. He yanked on her ears, punched her in the muzzle, and a new flood of pissed-off-ed-ness raced through me. No one hurt my psychopomp and got away with it.

The scythe read my mind. With a mighty roar, I aimed it at her grim and it sailed through the air, slicing into him—a guillotine at his neck.

For a half a beat, his face registered shock. Then he imploded, leaving only his robes and weapon behind. Ghost cocked her head, panted, and wagged her tail, untangling her paws from the fabric.

Without my scythe, however, I was no longer a ninja or action hero. The man under me punched me square in the nose.

My cheek stung and my jaw throbbed. Through blurry eyes, I saw Killion's claws rip through the mask his grim wore. His eyes glowed that bright red, his head twisting and his attention locking on me. He spoke but he was suddenly blotted out by my attacker, who rose up between us.

The flash of steel reflected in the sun. I knew the blow was coming before I saw him swing, and I instinctively shrank back.

Like magic, my weapon landed in my palm with a sharp sting. Ghost sprang, and I rolled sideways as the grim brought his blade down.

The screech as it struck the pavement reverberated around us like nails on a chalkboard. He raised his scythe again, but I was ready this time. Defending his next blow with a block, the impact of the blades shuddered through my body. Ghost barreled into him, knocking him sideways, but he was quick, twirling his weapon in his hand and nailing her abdomen.

The roar that came out of me deafened her own cry of

pain. "Come after me, that's one thing," I yelled, gaining my feet, "but two of you have now hurt my dog. *I will end you!*"

I lit into him with a ferocity I didn't know I possessed, taking him out at the knees. Stumbling, he fell into his buddy, bleeding profusely from Killion's claws. That guy caught his robes at the shoulder and tugged him forward. "Let's get out of here!"

The bubble that had surrounded us burst in a blaze of sparkling lights as they struck it with their weapons. Staggering, I started to go after them as they raced away, but a hand on my arm stopped me. "Let them go."

Killion was back to his normal self—completely unmussed and totally collected. No evidence of fangs or claws. While that was somewhat of a relief, it was also unnerving. How did he do that, and why did I want to throw myself into his arms? I stood wounded, heart pounding, and on the brink of vomiting, yet I could not tear my attention from him.

Ghost shrank to puppy size once more and danced at my feet. She had blood in her fur and the sight of it snapped me out of my Killion reverie and made me even more nauseous.

She wasn't the only one bleeding. Metallic flavor on my tongue, I checked my nose for busted cartilage and yelped when I hit a sore spot. "What just happened?" I spit blood onto the grass.

"Gustafson's followers. I warned you they would seek revenge."

"He tried to kill me! What was I supposed to do?"

"Technically, he *did* kill you." Killion examined my nose, then scrutinized my other injuries. "And if we don't succeed at training you to defend yourself, those reaper imposters will finish the job."

NINETEEN

Nita nearly dropped a plate of scones when we entered the coffee shop. Mason, a high school kid, had the morning shift with her today, but I saw no sign of him.

I assumed her reaction was because of my disheveled, bloody appearance, but her eyes locked on Killion. She paid no attention to me, nor the other customers lined up for their Saturday morning sustenance. A few in the younger crowd probably hadn't been home yet from a decadent night of partying. One or two of the older, more responsible, customers were on their way to jobs or their kids' soccer games, said children hovering around their legs and making tons of noise.

Killion and I snagged an empty table near the washroom. I placed Ghost, inside the duffle bag, under it, before I locked myself inside the cramped room with a single toilet, mirror, sink, and an overhead light that would make even the glamorous Jacqueline look like the living dead.

My nose and other injuries were healing, although the touch of the wet towel I used to scrub away blood still made me flinch as I washed certain spots. A minimal amount of bruising and swelling remained, but was fading fast. My watcher had explained that quick healing was now part of my norm.

Flashes of the scene I'd just survived reeled through my head, causing my body to tremble. I had a fresh laundry list of questions for him, and I wasn't going to let him blow me off this time.

Returning to the table, I found a plethora of food and drinks awaiting my tired, sore body. "You need to replenish your energy," he said, shoving a plate with assorted pastries at me.

Ghost hopped up on the seat next to my thigh. My pants were dirty and stained, a tear in the left calf. I was a mess, no two ways about it.

Normally, I'd try to hide the dog, since only service animals were allowed in the shop, but I pinched off a corner of the scone and fed it to her. No one seemed to pay much attention to us, and I was beyond caring. I broke off a larger piece for me and practically swallowed it whole. I was starving.

"Why did you save my life?" I asked around a mouthful. "In the alley Friday night?"

If he was taken off guard by my back-tracking, he didn't show it. "I suspected Gustafson was hunting. Your friend was a prime candidate. I was watching her, but was distracted by another...situation. When I picked up Darcy's trail again, I made my way to the alley. She passed me in a rush, looking terrified. I discovered you in the alley, having fought to the death with Gustafson. I felt that was my failing, and I wished to correct it."

Following the food with a gulp of iced caramel latte—extra whip, thanks to Nita—I processed that while I examined the dog to make sure she was okay. She must have had fast healing as well—there were no injuries left on her. "So, I'm not non-compliant, right?"

His shoulders moved in a shrug. "If you were, Jacqueline would have already paid you a visit."

My belly was growing happier by the mouthful. I ate and drank more, then continued my interrogation. "Why didn't I get a rush when I killed that grim?"

"Those imposters are human. As I mentioned previously, they're using blood magic to give them powers. Their souls are...tainted, you might say, because of it. His crossing, like Gustafson's, wasn't into the light."

"So hell exists, too?"

"They often end up in a version of purgatory."

Ghost demanded another piece of scone. I gave it to her and started in on a bowl of fruit and the muffin. "Are those two who were left going to try again? What exactly was that"—I wiggled a finger at his body—"that you morphed into?"

"Is that important? And yes, I suspect they will tend to their wounds and make a second attempt."

Awesome. "Are you going to eat?"

He seemed slightly awed, or possibly entertained, at my hunger. "I don't require sustenance at the moment."

"Why do I?"

"You are human."

Thanks, Captain Obvious. "And you're not?"

His gaze slid away.

Silence descended. A game, I suspected, him betting I would cave before he did.

I suck at holding my tongue, especially when hopped up on adrenaline. He won the bet. "Why did you let them go?"

He frowned and met my gaze over the table once more. "You and the dog were injured. While you fought well, you are untrained, and they had blood magic on their side, even if the two of us were superior to it. I could not risk further injury to you, nor to Ghost."

I rubbed an achy shoulder. The pain was already subsiding as we sat there. "Did you see how fast I healed?"

The safer subject brought his gaze back to mine. "A byproduct of the robes' magic."

So the robe had magic, too. Did everything? "I'm not wearing the robes," I countered. "I don't even have them with me."

"They are part of you, regardless." He toyed with a cup of coffee, but didn't drink. "The ones who attacked us were not reapers, only imposters. Groupies, you might call them. They desire to be grims and my investigation has revealed that Gustafson was training them and using dark magic to give them grim-like powers."

I thought this over as I chewed. "Can't the brass at SMG simply reap them and put a stop to their activities?"

He finally sipped his beverage and glanced around, making sure no one was listening. Nita, still working furiously, sent a warm appraisal his way, then arched one of her perfect brows in a clear *you've been holding out on me* message to me. "They are harder to find and stop than you imagine, which is why I've been trying to track them."

I took a big gulp of latte, licking whip from my lips and studying him. "In two days, I've taken out Gustafson and one of his followers. Me, a plain old *mundane*, who doesn't know what she's doing. Logic leads me to believe you haven't been trying very hard."

That got a bit of a rise out of him and I saw a flash of irritation in his eyes. "I assure you, no one is more surprised than I at your adeptness." His eyes were violet again and they did a slow perusal of my upper body. "You are... unique. An enigma."

Heat snaked up the back of my neck and down my cleavage, my tattoo tightening. Yet I wasn't sure it was a compliment. More as, he didn't enjoy puzzles, didn't appreciate me because I was one. I upset his world, and he didn't like being forced into fixing it.

I finished off the last of the muffin, brushing away crumbs to calm my racing pulse. "They attacked in broad daylight. What's wrong with them? Isn't there some kind of rule against that?"

"It should be obvious they don't play by our rules."

I liked how he said "our," as if I was part of this magical world. "Did you create the bubble so people wouldn't see what was happening? Was that the thing you call a glamour?"

A dip of his chin. "They are lost without their leader. Perhaps they are scrambling to find their next step."

Join the club. "Revenge seems high on the list." Ghost climbed into my lap and bedded down. I scratched her ears, relieved she was okay. Myself and Killion, too. "Have they been practicing on humans? Were they part of the serial killer attacks?"

"I believe the couple on your uncle's tables last night are a result of their work."

I'd entered the info into the hospital's system, flagging it to be shared with Detective Adams, the lead investigator, but there didn't appear to be any foul play. "The cause of death for each was heart attack."

Killion's long fingers snagged a strawberry from my fruit bowl. "Both healthy, young humans, experienced their hearts stopping at the same time."

It was said as a statement, but with an underlying question, mocking my intelligence quotient. "Agreed, it's highly improbable, but not impossible. Soulmates have been known to die in quick succession."

One brow arched. He ate the fruit. "You believe in such things?"

There was that touch of mockery again, but I watched carefully as he swallowed. Seeing him eat and drink had a mollifying effect on me. "My grandfather had a stroke and passed before an ambulance could arrive. Witnessing that created so much stress for my eighty-four-year-old grandmother, she had a heart attack and went, too. They found her slumped over his body, her hand entwined with his. So yes, I do believe in *that stuff*."

He said nothing, possibly to respect my grief, or more likely, because Nita rushed over at that moment. "Who's your friend?" she questioned me, while checking out Killion with a generous smile as she collected the dirty plates. Ghost let out a snore and her gaze dropped to my lap. "Is that a puppy? Oh my god, Chloe, when did you get a life?"

Across the table, Killion smirked.

TWENTY

"I have a meeting," he said, exiting his side of the booth. "Your training begins tonight. Wear attire you can move in easily."

Nita's mouth hung open as he bid her a good day and strode out. I started to jump up and grab him, but with Ghost sleeping in my lap, I stayed seated, not willing to disturb her. "I need a new manual," I called after him. "The dog ate mine!"

He ignored me and Nita slid into his vacated spot. She was taking her break, leaving Mason at the counter. He waved at me, as she began her interrogation. "Dish." Her fingernail tapped on the top of the table. "Who is hottie boy, and didn't you have a bloody nose when you walked in?"

I glared after my mentor's back, even though he'd vanished from view. "He's no one, and my nose is fine."

She glanced at the stain on my jacket and narrowed her eyes. "I may have only had a year as a med student, but I know a broken nose when I see it. You're lying."

"Okay, yes, it was bloody, but not broken. I don't know why. It's no big deal."

Her expression suggested she knew that wasn't the whole truth, but after scrutinizing my face, she let it drop. "He said you had *training* tonight. What does that mean? What manual?"

The remnants of my breakfast rested between us. The coffee, muffin, fruit, and scone were gone. The milk and juice nearly. The only thing left was a giant cookie—one of my favorites, too—a white chocolate fudge. "Did you tell him what I like?" I motioned at the stack of dirty plates.

"I didn't wait on him—Mason did."

He and I had worked together once or twice and said little beyond: "I need a dry short cappuccino with a shot of vanilla, and an iced brewed latte to go." So how had either he or Killion known my preferences?

"You've been holding out on me and I don't appreciate it." Nita gave me her pouty face. "Come on, Chloe. Tell me what's going on. Who is he and where did you meet him?"

Ghost whimpered in a dream. I stroked her head and she settled, giving me an idea. "The puppy is a rescue. I'm fostering her for now."

"That's great, but you know that's not what I was asking about. What's with the new boyfriend?"

I snorted. "He's not my boyfriend."

"Then what is he?"

I racked my tired brain for a proper term, but found none. It wasn't like "watcher" wouldn't require further definition and an explanation I couldn't give. "Mentor" would also bring up more questions better left unanswered. "We're acquaintances, that's all."

"Right, and this acquaintance is training you to do what, exactly?" Her eyes widened. "Wait, is this some kind of kink thing?"

I sputtered on a mouthful of juice and had to wipe my chin. "Don't be ridiculous. I'm learning self-defense." It was the first thing that popped into my head and was pretty close to the truth.

She leaned forward, inspecting my face as if she could read the lies written all over it. "Why? Did something happen?"

I decided to stay on this train, since it was working. "I had a run in with a bad character Friday night."

She hesitated, her face paling. "Oh my god, are you all right? Why didn't you tell me?" Leaving her seat to come around the table, she forced me to scoot over so she could sit next to me. "Chloe, what happened?"

I didn't go into detail, simply laying out the general facts about Miss Pickles and being attacked on my way home. "It's nothing, I'm okay." She grabbed me and administered a crushing hug as I tried to finish. "I simply decided I need to know how to defend myself."

"No wonder you haven't returned my texts." She looked me over again, brushing back a strand of hair from my cheek. "I can't believe you didn't say anything. Did you report the guy? Do you know who he is?"

I hated fibbing to her, but what could I say that wouldn't send her into full-on freak-out mode? "No. He disappeared when Killion showed up."

She pointed at the door. "That's Killion?"

I nodded and bit into the cookie.

"A Good Samaritan hottie. Girl, you better get some of that."

I choked again, this time on the cookie, and reached for the juice to wash it down. "That's so not going to happen."

"Why not? He's obviously into you."

"Oh, please. I'm definitely not his type. And he's not mine."

Her eye roll was classic. Mason called for help and she pushed out of the seat. "Fine, I need self-defense lessons. If you're not going after him, that is?"

She let the challenge linger between us. I knew exactly why she'd thrown down the gauntlet, attempting to get me riled up enough to make a move. I loved her, but she was a huge flirt, as well as a terrible matchmaker. I handed her the now empty glass. "I don't think he's your type, either."

"If he's single, breathing, and looks like that?" She hitched a thumb over her shoulder. "He's definitely my type."

At least she was honest. I slid Ghost off my lap and into the bag, trying not to jostle her too much. Completely tuckered out, she barely opened her eyes before snoring again. "I've gotta run. I'll text you later."

"Are we still on for test prep tonight?" she called on her way to the counter.

The anatomy test...I'd forgotten. Being attacked by a reaper could do that to you. "Of course."

"What about your training?" She winked conspiratorially, making air quotes.

Killion hadn't given me a time, and regardless of his suggestion I quit my jobs and drop out of school, I wasn't doing either. If I couldn't find a loophole and get out of it, this grim stuff had to take a backseat. "We'll work around it, but we are going to study. I'll let you know a time."

As she began helping customers, I shoved the last piece in my mouth. Then I hauled the bag strap onto my shoulder and left.

I tried not to be paranoid as I walked home, but every shadow made me jump. What if the grim wannabes came back? Ghost and I seemed to be a good team, but without Killion? I wasn't sure we could handle them.

I *did* need training. I had no idea what I was doing, and I refused to walk around in a constant state of fear. Whoever Gustafson's followers were—they were about to meet their match.

TWENTY-ONE

Vera was in the fenced backyard with her assortment of pets when I arrived. Her cockatoo, Petey, with his clipped wings, called to me as I came through the gate. An assortment of cats lounged in patches of sunshine, including Miss Pickles, who disdainfully glanced away with a lift of her nose when I said hello to her.

"Good morning," Vera called. A gardening apron wrapped around her ample waist, she waved a trowel in greeting. "How's the puppy?"

I set Ghost on the ground and she eagerly greeted the woman. Once finished, she ventured over to aggravate one of the cats. "Healthy and happy," I declared, thankful that was true. The little bugger was growing on me.

Vera tugged on a dead begonia and tossed the brown plant in a bucket. A gloved hand rubbed her chest. "Your shift went well?"

The two autopsies nagged at me. So did the thought of those grims attacking me again. Mostly, though, I kept reliving the moment with my mom. "Another quiet night," I lied. "How was yours?"

She drew an audible breath and bent over to close the hole. The birds chirped and golden rays of sunshine coming through the oak leaves colored the small space. "Pretty good."

That equated to meaning she was up a lot. I had a sneaking suspicion why.

But the scene was so normal, so comforting, I took a moment to simply stand there and not overthink it. Unfortunately, as I watched her slow movements and deliberate inhales, I had to pry. "Is your angina bothering you again?"

She waved off my concern, tiny dirt particles flinging from the trowel. "I'm fit as a fiddle. Have you had breakfast?"

I was stuffed and ready for ten hours of uninterrupted sleep. "I could use a cup of tea."

She anchored the tool on the edge of the flower patch and brushed off her gloved hands. "I could use one myself."

Inside her kitchen, I gathered tins of loose tea while she put water on to heat. I kept a close eye on her, listening to her breathing and noting that she rubbed her chest several times when she thought I wasn't looking. "Have you checked your blood pressure this morning?" I asked as casually as I could.

She sliced a lemon and placed the cheery yellow sections on a plate before carrying them to the table with two of her fancy cups and saucers. "You stop worrying about me, young lady." Cream came next, and at the sound of the fridge opening, all the cats came running, crying for a treat.

They scrambled around her feet, nearly tripping her, but she just chuckled when I scolded them. Ghost watched the circus with mild curiosity.

Bugging her would only make her angry and cause more

stress, so I kept the conversation on normal things for a few minutes, mostly nodding and stifling my yawns as she related various news stories, along with tidbits about the neighborhood.

After we finished our drinks and I finally begged off, I hoofed it up to my place with the dog. I took a moment to send her sister a message, informing her Vera was not feeling well, but refusing to admit it. A moment later, Velma let me know she would check on her and bring lunch, so Vera didn't have to fix any.

I was too exhausted to shower, so I slid between the sheets, not even complaining when Ghost burrowed down next to me. My leg banged into something hard, and I discovered upon inspection that there was a new manual on the bed.

Had Killion delivered it? Had that funny guy from this morning?

I'd have to worry about that later. I couldn't even hold my eyes open a minute longer and dropped like a lead balloon into sleep.

My dreams were filled with black robed beings. When I jerked awake sometime later, I found Death himself staring down at me.

TWENTY-TWO

"Eep!" Clutching the sheets, I scrambled across the bed, sending Ghost rolling off and landing on my butt on the other side.

My legs tangled in the bedclothes and I tossed about like a beached whale before I could regain enough balance to peek over the edge of the mattress.

Where Killion was all smooth, confident male, the guy grinning at me and petting my dog—who had jumped into his arms—was raw, carnal power. Raven black hair hung down to his shoulders, and his eyes snapped with a frosted green hue. Muscles bulged from every crack and crevice, and his brilliant white teeth flashed in the late afternoon shadows. "Hey, love," he said with a slight accent that was all butter-on-a-biscuit melty. Another Brit? Aussie? Porn star? "We were interrupted the other night. I didn't get to introduce myself. Thought it time I paid you a visit."

"You're..." I couldn't bring myself to say it, but the ugly word rang in my head and made my innards tremble. No psychic powers needed, I knew without a doubt that this was the Angel of Death in the flesh. Except, with those biceps and that devilish look on his face, he was no angel. "Are you here to...?" I drew a finger across my neck, indicating I was a dead woman walking.

Or perhaps more accurately, one who was crouching in fear. I'd never thought of death as a sentient being, outside of the way the grim reaper was portrayed in books, games, and movies, but every cell in my body knew I was looking at something far more deadly and destructive than a reaper.

"To kill you? Nah." He placed Ghost back on the bed. "But I have to say you really complicated things."

"I did?"

Swinging my desk chair around, he sat on it backwards, his muscled arms draping over the top rail. "Darcy was scheduled to die Friday night. Since you saved her, you should have died in her place."

My skin puckered in dozens of tiny goosebumps. "Well, that sucks."

"Killion, the fool, stepped in, and here we are."

He looked at me as though he expected me to nod or verbally confirm that I understood. I could only stare, my head feeling like a giant balloon losing air—I was supposed to be dead right now? My stomach was squishy and I covered my mouth with a hand. *Do not vomit!*

Squeezing my eyes shut, I held up a finger, silently indicating I needed a moment. Once my breathing returned to normal enough that I could speak, I swallowed the pit lodged in my throat. "You can't be in here. My landlady has a rule about no men in my apartment."

His brows drew together, forming a crease between them. "What is this, the 1940s?" He waved a finger through the air and a soft curtain of air fell like a bubble. "There, now she can't hear us."

Hopes of getting him out dashed, I frantically searched for another excuse, but found all I could do was gawk.

"So you see," he continued, apparently used to such a reaction, "the scales are unbalanced. Avi wasn't supposed to die."

My brain struggled to shift gears and decipher what he was getting at. "Who's Avi?"

"Grim 281. Avi Gustafson. Tinder explained all this."

"The guy at the shop?"

His eyes narrowed, as if he were trying to discern my IQ. "He made you sign the blood contract? Skinny guy, about so high?" He used a hand to estimate the man's height, far below his own. He had to be six-seven, maybe more.

"Are all of you British?"

Equal parts humor and concern over my lack of understanding danced in his eyes. "You don't like the accent? It's Aussie. Most women love it."

I fumbled with the sheet, making fists of frustration in it. "Gustafson was a serial killer. He deserved to die. What scales are you referring to? How are they unbalanced? Technically, I died, if only for a minute."

"Avi was a problem, yes, but moral issues aren't my department. However, as a grim, you are. As one of my reapers, you're going to help me recalibrate the scales, thereby saving the world of impending doom." He grinned.

Was he joking? I should have been more concerned with the doomsday threat but something else worried me more. "You're my...*boss*?"

The grin widened, and a sultry vibe, thick as molasses, rolled off him. *Yep, definitely porn star.* It tickled my skin. "Who did you think you were working for, love?"

I stuttered for a moment, blinded by the smile. "Uh...

that Soul Management Group? I did the contract thing, and they sent me an email. I have the manual." I pointed toward where the book had been, but it must have fallen off. "I thought that was the deal."

"Oh." He made a dismissive gesture. He dropped the accent as he continued. "Smudgy is more like...a board of directors. They handle all the soul stuff—birth, death, incarnation, reincarnation. Existentialism, philosophy, I could go on...but the *business* of death?" He cocked a thumb at his broad chest. "That's all me."

"Smudgy?"

"A nickname. They don't like it, but what do I care?" A wink. "I'm Death."

And I was screwed. "You all like nicknames, don't you? Tinder called me 'Grave Girl.'"

He glanced up, appearing to turn it over in his mind. "Catchy. I like it."

"Well, I don't. My name is Chloe, not babe, love, or Grave Girl."

"So we're good?" He nodded, blowing right over my statement. "You're all caught up?"

Untangling my ankles, I pushed myself up the wall, bringing the sheet with me. My gaze darted to the manual, which I could now see was lying on the floor. Ghost had made herself comfortable next to it and chewed on one corner.

"Bad dog." I retrieved the heavy thing, wiping drool from the pages. "Guess I missed the chain of command in the contract. This is all rather...mind-blowing."

"Killion didn't tell you about me? What a douche bag." Shoving out of the chair, he stood. "I'm not sure why he rescued you, but don't make the mistake of believing he's some savior. He's not. Part of your new position is going to be keeping your eyes and ears open, especially where it concerns him."

"Why is that?"

"Exactly. *Why* is what you should be asking yourself—why was he in the alley Friday night? Why did he resurrect you after you killed Avi?"

"He told me he's investigating the rogue reapers."

"Is he? Or is that an effective cover that allows him to keep their secrets and hide what they're doing?"

Ghost pawed at Death's leg. He hefted her up to scratch under her chin. "He could be their leader."

I toyed with the edge of the manual. "I thought Gustafson was."

"According to Killion, sure." He placed the puppy on the bed. "You took out the grim, who was a vampire, by the way. Killion set him up as the mastermind of all this. What if he's the mastermind?"

My heart sank a little. "But he's not a reaper. He's a..."

He cocked his head, waiting. When I didn't finish, he said it for me. "Vampire. A very old one, to be precise. An elder."

"You're trying to scare me. They aren't real."

"You're talking to Death, after learning that grims are actual entities, and you're denying vampires exist?"

I rubbed my forehead. "Santa Claus is real, too, I suppose?"

"He was once." His focus turned serious. Deadly so. "Wake up and smell the supernatural. The Undead exist. As do shifters, fairies, and a whole lot of other creatures the non-magical community doesn't believe in. You'll be reaping plenty of them, so you might as well get on board with it."

Vampires, shifters...my head spun. "Angels? Are they

real, too?"

He puffed up his chest. "What do you think, love?"

"I mean the good kind. With white wings and loving intentions."

"Wings are overrated."

Sucking in my bottom lip, I withheld comment. It also kept me from screaming and running from the room like a crazed woman. "I need time to adjust to all of this. It's a lot."

"Do you know what every vamp craves, Chloe?"

My worst fears about Killion's true nature confirmed, I swallowed the tightness in my throat. *They aren't real.*

The fangs had been. The supernatural strength, too. The lust for... My voice cracked. "Blood?"

Death stepped closer, eyes glittering as he leaned toward me. "Power. They think because they can delay death, they're more powerful than I am." Another smile split his face, but this one made the hair at the nape of my neck stand up. "Everything dies eventually." The weight of his words pounded against my skull and I backed up. "No matter how many of my grims Killion recruits, I'll be waiting for him. He'll never gain the power I have."

He seemed to want a response. My throat was tight, my body humming from his threat. "Um, I understand...?"

"Good. I want you to help me take him down."

"What?" I was backed against the wall, literally. I wanted to refuse, to argue. Killion might be an arrogant vampire—jeez, was I jumping over that hurdle now?—but he was also...

My friend. The thought weirded me out, but it was true. At least, I wanted it to be. Yes, he put out a jerk vibe at times, but he *had* saved my life. More than once. He was also the only one actually helping me adjust to my new grim status.

Bonus points: He'd ordered all my favorite foods after our run-in with Gustafson's crew.

When Death looks you in the eye and tells you to do something, however, it seems unwise to refuse. As his minion, I wasn't sure I could. "If I agree to this, what do I get out of it?"

He straightened and appraised me with renewed regard. "Negotiating, are we?"

It took everything I had to hold his actual "death" glare and force my trembling legs not to give out. If I didn't make a stand now, he would push me around for the next year. "I've killed a grim, died and come back to life, and fought off Avi's followers. The robes chose *me*. Regardless of Killion's involvement, and my limited experience, I'm *unique*." Using Killion's term gave me a burst of confidence. I stood taller. "You need me, or you wouldn't be here, wasting your valuable time. I have an in with him since he's my mentor. If you want me to use that to find out if he's your guy, then I want something in return."

Consternation, or something similar to what I'd seen on Killion's face multiple times in the past forty-eight hours, softened Death's features. "Your landlady has three days to live. I'll give her three more years."

I gulped. I'd planned to ask for something else, but considering my parents were already in the afterlife, he would probably tell me resurrection wasn't "his depart-ment." I pushed down my fear at losing the woman who was my surrogate mother. "Ten."

He cocked his head, delight on his face. "Five."

He liked a challenge. Fine. I'd give him one. "Seven." Was I really bargaining for her life? "If I get the proof you need, I want the full ten."

His lips twitched, amused. "Seven with a possible three-year extension, dependent on your performance."

"I want that in writing."

"Sure about that? You've never made a pact with me before."

A pact with the devil. That's what it felt like. "I'm sure."

"We do it in blood."

Great. I swallowed the lump in my throat. I may have been a vet tech, but seeing my own made me nauseous. "Works for me."

He flicked a finger toward my heart and a sharp sting bloomed on my chest.

"Ow!" Seven drops floated out from the wound and hung in the air between us. He reached out and grabbed them, the drops dissolving into his palm. Using a fingernail, he slit his own skin along his collarbone and droplets hovered in the air once more. "Eww. What am I supposed to do with those?"

He jerked my hand out and held it immobile as they made their way to me. His hand was bitterly cold, his dead energy seeping into my skin. One by one, they nestled into the palm and dissolved. I tried not to gag. "By the way, in order to correct the imbalances Avi and his followers have created, you'll need to round up the ghosts their kills have left earthbound."

My whole body vibrated and I felt dizzy. Good thing the wall was still behind me. I sagged against it, not sure if it was due to his blood or what he'd just said. "You've gotta be kidding. Ghosts?"

He strode for the door. "Those souls were victims, and it wasn't their time. Their contracts hadn't expired, and even though their bodies are out of commission, their souls are still tethered here. Shades need special handling."

"Shades?"

"That's what they're called."

"I don't see ghosts. How am I supposed to help them?"

He called me on my lie. "You saw Talon. Granted, he was a noncompliant—someone who's contract was up but was trying to dodge death. Shades are similar, only reverse—theirs isn't up but they die."

I'd also seen the ghost Killion had instructed me to leave for Jacqueline. "Okay, I may be able to see them, but I don't think I'm right for that job."

That garnered a full belly laugh, and it echoed in the apartment. Thank goodness for the quiet curtain. Vera would have a heart attack and die if she saw this guy in my place. "You're not *right* for this? Please, you made the decision to help that girl Friday night and here we are. You're what I've got. Start with the couple in the morgue. You'll find instructions in the manual."

"Why can't you question Avi? He's a ghost now, right? You could solve all of this with a conversation with him."

"Wish it were that easy. Vampires trade their souls for immortality. His spirit is on the other side in a place neither of us wants to visit. Even if I could talk to him, his soul checked out long before his undead body went rogue."

"Why a vampire? You obviously don't like them. I would think they'd be the last option on your list for a grim."

"You might be surprised. Vamps sometimes realize they made a mistake and ask for absolution. Not my department, you know, but Smudgy decided Avi could atone for his mistake and they hired him." He shrugged. "What are you gonna do? Didn't work out for either of us, I'm afraid, and I knew it wouldn't. You can't trust a vampire. Ever."

My stomach roiled. "But you're teaming up with one?"

"Beggars can't be choosers." He turned for the exit that

opened to the outside stairs. "Oh, and a suggestion—in the future, be careful with that free will you're throwing around like candy. Sometimes, it *bites* back."

Free will. Fate. My conversation with Killion circled my brain, as did the vision of his fangs.

Death was halfway out the door, Ghost whining at his departure. I ran after him. "I still want our deal in writing."

He didn't so much as look back. "Check the book, Grave Girl." Laughing, he faded away and disappeared.

I swung back, heart thudding. The booklet glowed with an eerie orange light. Opening it caused a series of pages to flip by, stopping on a blank one. As I watched in shock, words formed in gold, as if being written at that very moment. Like all contracts, it was full of legalese and convoluted phrases, but at the bottom, Death's name appeared, a droplet of blood next to it. My own handwriting formed my name next and another bloody dot soaked into the parchment.

I checked my fingers—they were all clean. This was pure magic.

What had I done?

Head spinning, I set it as far from me as possible before I flopped on the bed. How had my life gone from normal to bedlam so fast?

Ghost was ready for playtime and pounced on me. "I think I'm in big trouble," I said to her.

Jumping up and down on my chest, she wagged her tail and barked once, spittle flying. I closed my eyes and used my shirt to wipe my face.

Crawling back under the covers held great appeal, but before I could hide from the world, my blood tingled and a sharp knock sounded on my door.

TWENTY-THREE

When I threw it open and found Killion standing there in all his perfection, I was momentarily speechless. He was in a three-piece suit, hair styled, and smelling of his usual delectable scent, along with roasted coffee.

Seeing me half-dressed and disheveled, he seemed to be at a loss for words, too. Violet eyes roamed over me, taking in my t-shirt, boy shorts, and tousled strands. "When I said wear something comfortable, I meant workout clothes."

He seemed to be impeccable, day or night, except when he changed into his true monster form. I wanted to tell him about Death and his suspicions, but found myself tight-lipped about it. Motioning him in, I forced in a deep breath and focused on settling my racing pulse. After closing the door, I leaned on it, wishing I had more clothes on. Like a full, head-to-toe Teflon suit. Could fangs pierce that? I shivered at the memory of them. "We need to talk."

He held out the tall white cup he carried, the side emblazoned with "The Smoking Bean" logo and graphic design. "You do a lot of that."

I accepted the drink, peeling off the lid and inhaling the beautiful fragrance of coffee into my system. "And you don't do enough."

Restraint colored his expression. "As I've already expressed, you cannot get out of your contract. Accept it. We are wasting time."

"Patience is not your strong suit, is it? I'm not questioning my reaper status." I sipped the hot liquid, then crossed my arms over my chest. "We need to discuss the, uh, vampire in the room."

His gaze went wary. He didn't like being put on the spot. I expected him to dodge the subject, but after a significant pause, he nodded. "What is it you wish to know?"

Cooperation? My surprise was genuine. "You admit to being one?"

He didn't so much as blink. Maybe the Undead didn't need to, yet I swore he had previously. "I never denied it."

Death had said he was old, yet I would peg his age at no more than thirty. "When did it happen? The change,"—I motioned with the cup at him—"or whatever you call it."

"Does it matter?"

Stonewalling again. "Yes. Answer the question."

"You are suddenly demanding."

I stared him down.

An audible sigh parted his full lips. "I am descended from a vampire. My father belonged to a long bloodline from a foreign country and that family has existed for over five centuries. My mother, however, was human."

"Wow." I had no other words. Images of Dracula flitted across my mind. "Let me guess, there's a creepy castle in Transylvania with portraits of you in it."

"How did you know?" He gave me a slow, devilish smile.

"I can't tell if you're joking or not."

The smile broadened. A very rare sight indeed. "I like to keep you guessing."

Heat spread through my veins like a wildfire, but I grabbed hold of it and stuffed it in a deep hole. I had to clear my throat before I could speak. "You were born Undead? I've never heard of that. You weren't...you know...turned?"

At my fumbling over the correct term, the smile vanished. He looked as though he needed the caffeine worse than I did. "I have always been one."

"I hadn't realized vampires could reproduce naturally."

"It is rare for a human female to become impregnated by one of us, and more unusual for the child to live. I am an exception."

"The boy who lived."

"Excuse me?"

Or in this case, the vampire *boy who lived.* "Harry Potter." I waved it off and squeezed the bridge of my nose. "Never mind. I've been watching reruns on cable. How old are you?"

Deadpan, he said, "Too old for you."

"Eww," I said, faking disgust, yet another flashfire raced through me. I studied his eyes, that mouth, trying to see if he was teasing again. I. Could. Not. Tell. I mentally swore. "As if. I'm not into old dudes."

The lips twitched. "I assure you, you are safe from my advances."

Something in me felt disappointed at that. Relieved and offended, as well.

"Because I am both vampire and human," he said, "I age approximately ten human years for every one hundred. Therefore, I am thirty in human years, give or take a few."

Exactly what I pegged him to be. "Do you have a wife, kids?"

Everything in him went utterly still. The expression he gave me was a warning. "A wife and son. Both were human and perished in 1912 from influenza."

"I'm so sorry." I knew that look, that stillness bracing against the deepest of emotions—grief. "Losing those you love is the worst."

He nodded and relaxed again. Not completely, but enough to tell me he knew I understood, and appreciated my not prying any deeper.

I cleared my throat again, and glanced down at my toenails, painted a vibrant green shade called Toil & Trouble. I was long past due for a pedicure, but I'd sure hit the target with the toil and trouble part. "Just so I'm clear on the vampire rules: you can go out in sunlight? It doesn't fry you?"

"Over time, we develop the ability to handle it. Younger vampires must protect their eyes and skin, which is usually sensitive for decades."

"You don't eat food. You drink...blood?"

"When necessary, yes." At the face I pulled, he went on. "From willing donors. My nest—my current family— live peacefully with our human counterparts. We do not hunt them, like in the old days."

That was a relief. "Doesn't it get boring, only drinking blood?"

"I partake of a few favorite dishes on occasion. I enjoy coffee and wine."

We had that in common. "What do you sleep in?"

An eyebrow quirked, raising a lock of his dark hair that fell casually over his forehead. "Nothing."

"TMI!" I narrowed my eyes, visions of his naked self

bombing into my brain. Another thing to stuff in that hole. "I meant, do you sleep in a coffin?"

"That would be nonsensical. Vampires do not need sleep, but when we rest, most of us find beds much more comfortable and appealing."

Man, my hole needed to be deeper. Those images just kept coming. "I see." I sipped coffee, buying myself time to process all this. "What about bats?"

He visibly shivered. "Disgusting creatures."

"You don't...turn into one?"

"Should have seen that coming." He rocked slightly on his heels. "No, I have never shifted into a bat, and would not know how, even if I wanted to do so. That is Hollywood mistruth. I understand that the species is important to the environment, but they, how would you say it? Eww."

My thoughts exactly. "And you speak Romanian."

"*Da*, and several other languages."

That cleared up most of my questions for the moment. If only my head wasn't spinning again with all the info. "You feed the dog. I'll change."

I left him to figure out where the kibble was stored—the kitchen wasn't big—and shut myself inside my tiny closet. Stripping down, I considered grabbing a quick shower, but 'training' meant hot and sweaty calisthenics. No point in wasting time—or having those images of Killion naked— haunting me while in there.

My workout clothes were buried in a pile of clean laundry I hadn't bothered to hang up or put away. They were on the very bottom, owning to the fact my exercise schedule was like my social life—pretty much non-existent. Since bending to touch my toes was an epic event, I worried I'd make a fool of myself. The fact I'd fought off two men— magical or otherwise—in the past few days had to be a fluke.

A pair of yoga pants, a tank top, and a worn sweatshirt with Baby Yoda on it later, and I was dressed. I finger-combed my hair into a ponytail and grabbed my bag.

The scythe was inside on the bottom. The robes lay draped over my school backpack. I picked the fabric up and checked for signs of life.

My parents took me to SeaWorld when I was nine. I had a fascination with marine animals then. I thought becoming a marine biologist was my path, even though we were landlocked in the south. I was fascinated with rays, dolphins, and whales at the theme park, and I spent a solid hour at the open ray tank, where the harmless creatures swam endless circles and we were allowed to put our hands in to touch them.

Their skin was the weirdest thing I'd felt up to that point, cool beyond measure. The texture was alien, rubbery, and made me want to pull my hand away, and yet not. The fabric of the robes had a similar consistency. It was foreign to my senses, like something not of this world, and yet, I couldn't stop stroking it.

I worried a sleeve between my finger and thumb and held it up to the dim overhead light. The cloth was thick, a web of magical threads, and I wondered for the hundredth time why it had chosen me.

Death's suspicions teased at my brain. Maybe Killion had said that to plant the idea in my head, to make me feel special, and at the same time, to lock me into needing his advice and direction. If he was the insider Death believed, he could manipulate me and turn me into his own personal weapon.

Shifting several shoe boxes aside, I found a damaged blue one on the bottom. Lifting the lid, I eyeballed the contents. Once my father saw how uncoordinated I was, coupled with my lack of interest in self-defense, he'd outfitted me with multiple non-lethal weapons. While I routinely carried the pepper spray, I'd never made use of the others. They were heavy to carry, along with books and my laptop when I went back and forth to campus.

Now, I added one to the bag and tucked a smaller version in my jacket pocket. I didn't know who I could trust, but it was long past time I listened to my instincts.

Returning to the cramped living area, I found Killion and Ghost waiting for me. Both appeared happy to see me—the dog, ready to go on an adventure; my mentor relieved I had proper attire.

I hefted the bag's strap onto my shoulder. "Ready when you are."

TWENTY-FOUR

The sun was sinking, reminding me of our early morning walk, complete with shadows creeping across the path.

This time of day, however, there were plenty of people out and about. Kids played soccer in the street. Adults were mowing lawns filled with fall leaves. Doorways and yards were decorated for Halloween.

"Where are we going?" I tried to sound casual. Ghost wanted down but I kept her close, fearing an attack.

"To a place with the equipment we need." Killion's long legs ate up the sidewalk and I had to hurry to keep the pace. Those who noticed us moved out of the way. "You need to learn how to use your weapon properly."

I felt pretty sure the scythe had its own ideas about that. "Do the grims have a boss?" Couldn't hurt to feel him out about Death. See what he could tell me about him. "I know SMG is in charge of the overall, uh, business of death, but is there someone I have to report to for assignments?"

"You've already met."

How did he know?

He glanced at me from the corner of his eye as we rounded the corner onto Fayette Street. "You stink of him."

I lifted an arm to sniff my pit. I didn't smell fresh, but I couldn't discern any noticeable fragrance of my earlier visitor. I sighed. "He just barged in. You could've warned me about him, you know."

"No fun in that."

Was Mr. Stoic making another joke? Ghost wiggled in my arms, straining toward him. She was such a traitor. "Thanks for leaving me unprepared. Waking up to the sight of him watching me sleep took ten years off my life."

"I hope the deal you made with him is worth it."

"Reading my mind again? Boundaries, dude." A trace of jealousy had laced his tone. That gave me pause. Not that it was any of his business, but... "My landlady was supposed to die in a few days. I bought her more time."

"In exchange for what?"

We neared the alley where I'd taken out Gustafson. A shiver ran through me. Should I tell him or not? I stewed, glancing down the alley. "Did you know him? Avi?"

Killion, already past the entrance, halted with his back to me. "No."

"But he was a vampire, like you."

"We didn't run in the same circles."

Okay, then. In a small town such as ours, how were there enough supernaturals—particularly the undead variety—to form *multiple* circles? "You're sure he was the leader of the rogue reapers?"

Killion pivoted and doubled back to me. "Evidence suggests so." His head cocked ever so slightly. "Why?"

My favorite question right now. "Death wants me to look into it." I observed his face carefully to catch any reaction. "See if there may have been someone else in charge."

The half-truth might tip him off, but also potentially put pressure on him. That could work in my favor.

The corner of his mouth quirked. "He asked you to investigate it, didn't he?"

"Don't look so amused. Is that hard to believe? That he thinks I have the skills?"

He gave a light tug to my jacket sleeve. "Come on."

As we continued to the south side of town, the houses became older versions, lots of 1960s ranches that were rundown, the yards nearly non-existent and dry, orange clay peeking through bare spots. Decorations and ornamentation here dwindled as well, but there were plenty of folks out on stoops and huddling together on the corners.

We passed a convenience store and an apartment complex, cutting through a pawn shop parking lot and moving into a stretch of row houses. As we approached an abandoned Catholic church, Darcy materialized out of a bar with three other college students. Country music and TV noise was cut off abruptly when the worn wooden door swung shut behind her. "Oh, hey y'all," she called. "What are you doing out here? Slumming, Chloe?"

Her companions barely glanced at us, heading for a scuzzy looking van. I didn't recognize any of them, but I did know the type—dropouts, misfits, trouble. She sure seemed to have a knack for finding it. I wondered if Larson was in the bunch.

Glittering strings of beads hung around her neck, her eyes unfocused and glassy. The alcohol fumes coming off her were enough to make my head spin. I held my breath. "Hi, Darcy. Are you okay?" At her blank look, I clarified. "From Friday night. In the alley?"

The blank façade stayed that way. "What alley?" Her loopy gaze swung to Killion. "Hi there, handsome."

He nodded politely, his eyes tracking the other three at the van. They were watching us. "Would you like us to escort you home?"

"Home? Don't be silly. The night is young." She stumbled closer to me, lowering her voice as she slung her arm around my shoulders. "He's kinda old for you, isn't he? I mean, he is hot, but..."

She snort giggled and swayed. I grabbed her arm to steady her. Did she really not remember Friday night? I glanced at Killion, but his face was neutral. "I better make sure she gets home."

A black limo with a gold dragon hood ornament wheeled into the parking lot, the streetlights—at least, those were still working—reflecting off the high gloss. "My driver will escort her."

Darcy made a disgruntled noise. "I'm not going..." The instant the vampire touched her, her eyes rolled up in her head. Boom, she dropped like a rock, yet landed softly.

"Hey," one of the guys yelled. "What are you doing with her?"

Killion scooped her up in his arms and carefully tucked her into the backseat in one fluid motion. He closed the door and muttered something to the driver through his open window, then turned to face the three men now strutting toward us. Violence was in their walk. "Turn around and leave," he commanded in a voice that brokered no argument. "And stop preying on young women."

The limo drove off. I tensed, preparing myself for a tussle. Ghost growled softly.

All three paused, their gazes going flat. Their facial features and stiff postures softened. One by one, they pivoted, strolled back to the van and got in.

"Shazam." I grinned. "Can you teach me how to do that?"

"I suspect you already can."

My mind tripped back to the trio I'd encountered on the sidewalk. Double shazam. "Like on anyone? I can simply tell them what to do?"

He made a noncommittal sound and watched the van drive away.

I had to try my new power out, but later. "Whatever voodoo that was, why didn't you use it on our attackers today?"

"Drunk humans are easier to manipulate."

Didn't exactly answer my question, but apparently rogue grims intent on murder were not as easy. I thought about it, and decided that even if I could get people to do what I wanted, I didn't want to. Most of the time, anyway. That was an invasion of privacy, and interfering with their free will. I didn't want mine taken away, which it sort of had been. I wasn't about to do it to others.

He started for the rundown church and I trailed behind. "If you have a limo, why are you making me walk?" I stopped short, a former parking space painted line seeming to glow under my feet. My vision turned slightly gray, like a filter had suddenly covered my eyes. The church glowed as well. "You wanted to see if those guys would come after us again—the fake reapers—didn't you?"

He glanced at me over his shoulder. "Why would I do that?"

Uh, let's see. Because you're into manipulating humans? "That's the kind of training you had in mind, isn't it? Easy enough to use me as bait."

He whirled and returned to me, looking like a thundercloud. "I would never put you at risk." His eyes bore into mine. "You walk everywhere. I assumed you like doing so."

I rubbed at my eyes, trying to get rid of the gray, cobwebby filter the church seemed to put on everything. Was he saying he walked with me to make me...*happy?* "I don't have a car, Killion, and I try not to spend too much money on rides. I'm a broke college student, in case you haven't figured that out."

He looked perplexed for a moment. His voice was tinged with disappointment. "I've rather enjoyed our jaunts."

Surprisingly, I had, too. Except for the being attacked part. "Just so we're clear, I'm totally down with a limo ride any time you want to offer one."

"Noted." He began moving away again.

"What kind of magic is in this place?" I glanced around at the glowing building. "It's making my vision wonky."

His glance was mildly surprised. "You can see it?"

"Yeah." And the other thing I could see made me gasp. "Dude, what are *those?*"

The church had an old cemetery off to the north, the gray headstones and crumbling monuments brighter than the surrounding lawn that had gone to weeds. Around one of the largest crypts, spectral figures with red eyes and fangs hovered, gnashing their teeth. Their elongated muzzles sniffed the air in my direction.

Ghost bristled and growled, tiny but fierce.

Killion followed the direction of my gaze. In an instant, he was at my side. He grabbed my hand and yanked me toward the entrance, a statue of the blessed mother tipped slightly and wearing a strand of beads, as though drunk herself. "Get inside."

TWENTY-FIVE

The ornate wooden double doors had iron hinges and adornments straight out of the middle ages. The detailed structure towered over us and I swear it felt like generations of souls and saints were staring down at me. Not to mention the gargoyles perched on the roof's corners.

Each of the doors displayed a dragon's head knocker with a heavy ring through the mythical animal's nose. Killion used the right hangar to bang on one. "Katarina, open up."

A glance over my shoulder toward the cemetery beasts made me nearly throw myself at the entrance. Edging around the corner of the building, they growled and snuffled as they limped toward us. "You can enter this place?"

A peephole, hidden in the left side, slid open, a heavily lined and long-lashed green eye peeking out. "About time."

"Good evening," Killion said to her, and then to me, "Why wouldn't I?"

A series of clunks and clanks came from the interior. The beasts picked up speed. Ghost's hackles rose and she came to attention in my arms.

I reached for the stun gun in my waistband. "Because you're a vampire and the whole crucifix/consecrated ground/holy water stuff. Can we hurry this up?"

The last bolt clicked, and the door began to slide open. The beasts neared the Virgin Mary, knocking her the rest of the way to the ground as they lunged in unison for the steps.

I screamed, Ghost bolted from my grasp, and an iron grip lifted me from the ground by my jacket before I could zap the closest monster. Its razor sharp teeth raked my shoe, however, and a spike of pain drove into my big toe.

As I was unceremoniously hauled backwards into the church, Ghost morphed into her psychopomp form, and the graveyard beast's head was torn clean off.

"Bad dog!" Our hostess swore, dumping me on the tiled floor. "You leave my babies alone!"

Killion grabbed Ghost's collar, the second attacker retreating as Katarina snapped her fingers and sent it to the cemetery, once more with its tail between its legs. She stared down at the beheaded thing on the steps and shook her own. "No treats for you," she scolded Ghost, ignoring the psychopomp's deep throated growl. Dog and woman stood nearly eye to eye. Katarina scratched under her chin. "Do that again, and you'll be dog stew, hear me?"

"Hey now." I gained my feet, the smell of dry rot and ancient oppression strong in the interior air. "Your ghouls attacked us. She was defending me."

One of those cool green eyes slid my way. Slowly, she pivoted to look at me full on. She was taller than me, thanks to her heeled boots, and there was an odd energy around her. I felt itchy under my skin, my pulse jumping. "This is the new one?"

The scythe whispered in my head, *Kill.*

Killion shoved the heavy door closed, then brushed his hands together. "She needs extensive training."

And hopefully not from you.

In the candle lit room, shadows danced like a specter on the towering walls and the tiled floor. The dome ceiling echoed back her words, as if ghosts mimicked us. She sniffed and screwed up her nose. "But she's human...and..." Another sniff, her face contorting in horror. "You've shared blood with her?"

Killion's gaze went steely. "It is mine to give."

She bowed her head, then shot me a glare.

Now my hackles rose. "You have a problem with humans?"

Her raven black hair, matching lipstick, and multiple piercings gave her the appearance of an aging goth desperately clinging to her rebellious youth. Her lips curved in a savage grin and she chucked me under the chin. "I eat them for breakfast."

Gulp.

I seriously did take a second to swallow hard. "I kill grims." I raised a defiant chin. "The robes chose me."

Her lips trembled from holding back a laugh. She glanced at Killion. "She's got pluck, but are you sure she's worthy?"

"Worthy of what?"

Striding toward a desk in her thigh-high boots, her short skirt fluttered in the breeze her swift movements created. Ghost began to shrink and the vampire motioned me to follow.

Was our host one of his *kind?* I had no idea how to tell. She wasn't sporting fangs at the moment, but neither was Killion. At a giant mahogany desk in a secluded alcove, surrounded by shelves of ancient texts and burning candles, she lifted a feathered quill pen, dipped it in a pot of dark liquid, and handed it to me. "Sign your name, reaper."

Seeing the candles and all that old paper struck me as a test of fate, but the church had stood this long, and I didn't see scorch marks anywhere. As she slid an open book with pages of parchment around, she indicated a line, and I saw above it were other names, some in elaborate script, others simple black Xs. I hesitantly accepted the quill, a bead of the liquid wiggling on the metal tip, about to fall. "What is this?"

"A legacy." She peered from under her dark bangs, the hint of challenge in her eyes. "Only the chosen are allowed into the chamber."

I was pretty sure I didn't want to know what happened in there. "Chamber? Like as in secrets?"

Her head tilted. In confusion? Annoyance? It was difficult to tell.

"Harry Potter?" I clarified. "The Chamber of Secrets?"

Those killer eyes dismissed me and flicked to Killion. "You didn't tell her?"

Ghost scratched at my leg, back to puppy size and wanting up so she could see what was going on. As I glanced at Killion, I blinked. For a beat, he seemed to glow. It wasn't the same as what I'd observed outside, but it was... something. Silvery and shimmering.

Before he replied, the drop of ink—or whatever it was—fell, splashing on to the parchment. The paper immediately soaked it up and, as it disappeared, my name appeared in its place.

Katarina plucked the quill from my fingers, expression dumbfounded. "You *are* worthy. Please." She waved a hand toward the dark hallway, lit only by flickering wall sconces. "Proceed."

Killion strode past us, no longer glowing, and I picked up Ghost and hurried after him. "Wait. I thought we were going to a gym to work out and practice self-defense. What is this place?"

With a wave of one hand, he sent a set of stained wooden doors, similar to the entrance, swinging open. Carved into the giant doors was a depiction of the Archangel Michael, sword in hand, striking down a dragon. An assortment of other animals seemed to side with the creature—bears, wolves, lions.

"Whoa." The word tumbled out, sounding small and insignificant, as we entered a room twice as large as the foyer.

"Why doesn't Darcy remember Friday night?" I asked, turning in slow circles as I took in the splendor.

"SMG may have sent a cleaner to erase her memories of it. If she'd reported the attack, and your involvement in it, things would be messy with law enforcement."

Cleaners...another thing to learn more about.

Marble pillars supported the arched ceiling and were kitted out in gold. Multiple balconies loomed on both sides over various equipment and machines spread in an arc around the sizable perimeter. I wasn't sure if they were torture instruments, or someone's idea of antique collectibles, but surely they weren't anything you would find at a normal place of worship. Or a gym for that matter. At the far end was an altar and a towering golden statue. "Is this the nave?"

Ghost catapulted from my arms and ran to sniff one of the contraptions. Killion continued toward the altar, separated from the long, rectangular room by a narrow carpeted step and a railing. "Yes, but not in the sense you're thinking."

I wasn't sure what I was thinking, and noticing what waited for us on each side of the statue, I had to blink again.

Two men bookended its feet. As the vampire drew near, they began to struggle. Their hands and feet were bound, their mouths working, but no sound emerged. Eyes as big as saucers, they both watched him stop and turn back to me. "This is a place out of time, although still bound to the earth. We use it for things such as this...training and other *delicate* missions."

I'd stopped about halfway up the former aisle, the shadows from the dozens of flickering candles making me uneasy. Feeling watched, I glanced up at the balconies, but other than more shifting shadows, I saw nothing. Only empty chairs and darkness. "Who are they and why are they here?"

The men had been so focused on Killion, they'd paid no attention to me. Now as I stepped closer, their terrified gazes shifted in unison. They looked shocked and renewed their struggles as I grew closer. Their soundless mouths formed screams.

"Do you not recognize them?" Killion asked.

I peered at each man and my blood warmed, my pulse skipping. Ghost came running, seeming to sense my distress.

Previously, they had been masked, but as recognition dawned, my palm heated with a white hot flash, itching for the scythe. The two screaming men were our morning attackers.

TWENTY-SIX

I didn't like the way Killion stared at me. He motioned at the pair with one hand. "They're all yours."

"You want me to...?" I couldn't finish the sentence. "No way. I'm not going to kill them."

Pausing, he appeared amused. "At present, we need to interrogate them. I assumed you would want to be here for it."

While he wasn't ordering me to end their lives, I had the uncanny sense his idea of interrogation differed from mine. "Of course." I chuckled, embarrassed. "Good idea." I could uncover the truth about their leader, get Death off my back, and clear the vampire's name—if Killion was truly innocent. Switching my gaze from his to the frightened men, I held up my hands in a placating gesture. "I won't harm you if you cooperate, okay?"

One wore an eye patch, the other had a heavy mustache. Their mouths closed and they glanced around, as though looking for some way to escape.

The woman in plaster—Saint Ann?—stared down at us

with gentle, benign eyes. Funny, since earlier I would have sworn she'd been looking out over the vast space where a congregation had once gathered.

Some type of conclusion reached after the two exchanged a glance, Eye Patch nodded.

"Great," I said, facing Killion again. "Take off the magical gags, will you?"

He waved a hand and the men instantly started babbling. My palm still burned and itched. I ignored it and the wiggle from my bag where the scythe threatened to break free. Setting everything on the floor, I raised my voice to be heard and ordered the two to hush. "One at a time, and only in response to our questions."

Ignoring me, their words echoed in the space as they tried to talk over each other. It was astounding how loud two people could get.

Like buzzing bees, the noise grated on my nerves, my hearing suddenly extra sensitive. "Enough!" Now my voice pinged off the walls and ceiling, reverberating back to me.

They still didn't listen, their declarations climbing another notch, competing with mine and each other's. Each man seemed to be on a tirade about the partner I'd killed.

When I turned an exasperated face to Killion, he simply leaned on the rail, appearing amused. With a gesture that seemed to say, "It's your show," he waited.

Training. I'd assumed there would be a physical component, but getting information from suspects and conspirators was probably equally important. This was part of what I had to learn.

I had seen plenty of Law and Order reruns, but I was tired. They tried to kill me earlier and had few rights in my book.

Withdrawing the stun gun from my waist, I held it up. I didn't raise my voice this time, but took the opposite approach and lowered it. "I will put as many jolts as possible in your chest if you don't shut up."

Amazingly, it worked. Sudden silence left a void in the nave. *That's better.*

When I glanced at my mentor this time, he smirked. "Not exactly protocol, but seemingly effective."

High praise. "You have protocols for this kind of thing?"

He pushed off the railing. "Tell us who else is in your group," he demanded from our grim wannabes.

Another glance passed between them, but they had clammed up good. I brandished the weapon and stepped closer. "Talk, or else."

"You don't want to mess with them," Eye Patch said, his voice hushed.

The other man stared at me, the wooly caterpillar on his upper lip quivering as he spoke. "You've already upset them. Taking out Gustafson was a mistake. Best you crawl into a hole and hide."

It wasn't the implied threat so much as the way he said it that sent a shiver of fear through me. "No can do. I'm claustrophobic." It came out snarky, but it was true. Night-mares about being buried alive had haunted me since I was a kid. My hamster died and we put him in the backyard. Afterward, I kept having dreams that he was still alive, trapped in that box. "Tell us who your leader is."

Mustache looked at the floor, Eye Patch slitted his gaze to the side.

Killion showed no emotion, but since he rarely did, that didn't confirm whether he was or wasn't their boss.

I flipped off the safety guard on the gun. "I want a name."

Eye Patch shifted, eyes half-darting to Killion, then away. Mustache acted like it was all he could do not to spill his guts.

Were they covering for Killion? I didn't want to juice them, but I would. "So you're willing to face torture rather than share who recruited you?"

"We were promised powers," Eye Patch whined. "Burpee wasn't supposed to die."

"Burpee?" Killion asked.

Eye Patch nodded, and jerked his chin my direction. His lone eye studied me. "The guy she killed this morning."

I kicked one of his feet. "I don't care what Gustafson promised you and Burpee. Who is the head of your group? Give me a name and I'll let you go."

Killion frowned at me. He obviously had no intention of releasing them.

Neither did I, in actuality, but they didn't know that. Maybe I didn't need training—maybe those reruns had actually done some good.

Mustache shook his head. "We can't tell you, no matter what you do to us."

A strange, high-pitched noise hit my left ear. I jiggled my lobe and worked my jaw, trying to pop and clear the ringing from it.

On my left, Killion showed his fangs and a chill lanced down my spine. "You might want to rethink that."

The sharp ringing intensified. Eye Patch's body began to tremble. Mustache screwed up his face. "Too...late...," he gasped.

I glanced at Killion, holding a hand over my ear. "Do you hear that?"

His face contorted and he nodded. The frequency

jumped another notch. Reaching for me, his violet eyes darkened in what looked like fear. "Get down!"

Above us, Saint Ann exploded.

TWENTY-SEVEN

A chunk of plaster slammed into my head. Crying out, I tumbled to the floor with Killion on top of me, covering my body with his.

The shrill screech coming from the statue deafened me, dirt and more of the concrete pieces raining down on us. Hands over my ears did no good, the shriek twisting its way into my brain. A warm trickle of blood ran into my eye and I swiped at it. The scent of warm caramel and old libraries filled my nostrils.

Oh god. It was Killion's, not mine. His body was a dead —or *un*dead—weight on me. I gave a shove, my breath crushed in my chest, but couldn't shift him aside. The temperature felt like it had dropped ten degrees. "Killion," I cried, my voice barely audible above the shrieking. "*Killion!*"

No response. Surely he wasn't actually *dead.* My vision blurred, thanks to the dust in my eyes, my head pounding from the blow. Straining, I reached both arms around him and hugged him in an attempt to roll him off. They touched a smooth instrument protruding from his back.

Lifting my head to peer over his shoulder, I blinked to clear my eyes—gold and white colors blurred and blended. What was that? It certainly wasn't plaster. I ran my fingers over the cool outline of it and gasped.

It was the cross from Ann's neck.

The long end was embedded at heart level, a perfect hit. Vampires...stakes...

I bit my tongue to keep from retching and dug in my heels, gripping the thing to pull it out. "Hang on," I told his slack face.

Nothing changed on his countenance. The unusual weapon was lodged deep and wouldn't budge.

"Don't you dare die on me," I ground out, my voice a dim buzz against the backdrop of the continued ringing in my ears. I slapped at his cheeks, pinched his side.

Nothing.

When a second tug didn't work, I shoved again, getting my hips into it. This time, I managed to shift his legs, and their weight pulled his pelvis to my left. One more rock and roll and my lower half was free.

I still couldn't bring things into focus, but I called for Ghost, praying she was okay. Her tiny head appeared above my face and she licked my nose. "Help me," I ordered.

She chomped down on Killion's shoulder, using his clothing to tug. Breathing hard and calling on all of my strength, I shoved once more and the two of us slid his upper body off mine.

My limbs trembled and hummed. My blood raced in my veins. I scrambled to all fours, swayed, and nearly tossed my cookies. The combo of my apparent head injury and seeing the blood coming from his chest made it hard not to.

Straddling his back, I grasped the arms of the cross and

yanked with all my might. My hands were slick with blood and slipped, the wood itself freezing cold. I tumbled backward and threw out a hand to keep myself upright. Wiping my palms on my pant legs, I stared at the weapon, wondering how I could pull it out. More importantly, was it already too late?

Ghost danced around his head, barking at me and licking his face. Swearing commenced as I locked onto the bloody thing once more. Frosts did not give up when someone needed them. I dug my knees into the vampire's sides and yanked with all my might.

Resisting my strength, it stayed buried. Frustrated tears threatened to leak from my eyes. "Some saint you are," I yelled at the portion of Ann's face lying a few feet away. Anger churned in my belly alongside the nausea.

I grabbed the arms of the pendant and gritted my teeth. The few occasions my dad tried to teach me self-defense, he'd told me to yell or grunt with every strike. Something about helping me exert more power. If ever there was a time I needed to channel it, now seemed like it. Squeezing my eyes shut, I let a sound rise from the depths of my belly where that anger burned and heaved.

The sucking noise it made as it slid out of Killion was sickening. My chest gave a sigh of relief, as if it had been buried in my heart instead. Unfortunately, when it did let go, I lost my balance and tumbled backward, the heavy ornament whacking me in the forehead.

I hit the floor, groaned from the added abuse, and hurled it as far as I could. Which wasn't much. It landed a few feet away with a clatter. Staring up, the high ceiling seemed to sway overhead. I blinked, trying to get it to stop.

I heard a gurgling noise nearby. I rolled to my side and

came up on all fours, reaching for him. "Killion? Are you alive?"

A grunt was all I got in response. His fingers twitched.

That was enough. Hysterical laughter bubbled from my throat, but before I could celebrate, the lights flickered and went out.

TWENTY-EIGHT

My already bad vision was now useless. In the cloying darkness, I ran my hands over Killion, working my way up his muscled leg, back, and then finding an arm. I yanked off my shirt, glad for the tank top underneath, and pressed it against his wound. Sticky blood leeched between my fingers.

Blind, my hearing became more acute. The ringing in my ears was only a background noise. My own labored breathing assaulted my eardrums and I leaned over Killion to see if I could hear any further mumblings or feel him move. Neither happened, but I sensed a being to my right. "Ghost?"

I heard her growl, low and vicious, and the hair on the nape of my neck rose. I groped for her. "Come here, girl. What is it?"

She had morphed into psychopomp. Her fur was wet to the touch. I blinked, willing my eyes to adjust, but nothing changed. It seemed unnatural, this complete blackout—magic of some sort? "Katarina? Where are you?"

The swish of fabric and the faintest rustle of air touched

my face. My ears cleared. Everything in me went very still and my skin pebbled from the cold. Ghost's body was so tense, it quivered under my fingers.

Don't move. I prayed the dog understood.

The zing of a blade cut across the silence, coming from the spot where I'd left my bag. I swiveled in that direction, my blood suddenly hot in my chilled veins. I sensed something change with Killion, but I had to focus on who—or what—had just picked up my scythe.

"Who's there?" I addressed the darkness, pulse beating furiously. "What do you want?"

The only answer was a deafening silence. I wiggled my ears again, which seemed to defy me. Whoever it was had caused the eardrum-blowing frequency, the explosion, and the blackout. Now, he was hunting.

I struggled to control my racing heartbeat and to quiet my heavy breathing.

"No," I heard Eye Patch whine. "Please don't. We didn't tell her any—"

The blade let off a flash of light as it streaked through the darkness. His words died on the air. A sickening thud followed as his head hit the floor.

His friend screamed, the pitiful cry cut off a second later, when his head was also disconnected from his body.

I shook Killion hard. "Wake up," I whispered. "I need you."

Another rush of heat seared through my veins and I felt the urge to scratch my arms, legs, belly. The stench of death filled the air, the odor of fresh blood mixing with the ancient scent of this place. The man wielding my scythe neared on silent feet. I could sense him, like maggots crawling over my skin.

"You're the one," I murmured, rising. Still wrapped in

darkness, I dared not step forward, afraid I'd trip. "You're the rogue grim."

My palm itched so fiercely I had to scratch it. The call of the blade echoed in my bones. It wanted me to stop this creature, but I didn't have the faintest clue how. Then again, I hadn't known how to kill a grim before, either.

Ghost pressed against my leg. The two dead souls weren't crossing, I guessed, since she stayed to protect me. In the distance, I heard what sounded like a plague of locusts descending on the church.

The being paused, listening.

The fire inside me burned hotter, brighter, and I felt a rush of courage. I was not about to be killed by my own blade, but if I did nothing, my head was going to roll, along with the others.

The din of footsteps sounded on the high roof. The air was rent by a mighty roar—not from Ghost, but from the vampire at my feet.

The noise curled around my toes and set the rogue reaper in motion.

The blade flashed again as he raised it to swing, illuminating a masked face covered by a hood. The robes whispered to me as the scythe came at my neck. Ghost barked and leaped as I lifted an arm to block it.

Before the metal made contact, a strong hand grabbed my ankle and jerked it out from under me. I went sprawling. Dozens of creatures crashed through the windows and poured through the double doors.

The scythe fell to the floor, clattering, and a semblance of light returned. In the next heartbeat, the rogue reaper vanished and vampires, wild with rage, descended on me.

TWENTY-NINE

Claws ripped through my clothes and tore into my legs, arms. Fangs flashed and I felt the scrape of them on the sensitive skin of my neck.

My screams were drowned out by the mob. Lifted into the air and jerked this way and that, I feared my limbs would be torn from my torso.

"Stop!" A voice boomed, the same amplified one I'd heard Killion employ earlier. The rafters shook with it, the sound rattling inside my head. If I hadn't been fighting for my life, I might have cowed.

The other vampires did. In the same fury as they had descended on me, they freed me, my poor body falling to the floor like a dead weight.

The jarring knocked the breath from my lungs and I laid there for several frantic heartbeats, trying to get it back. Everything in me hurt and I couldn't find the strength to move.

"Help her up," Killion commanded, causing my extremities to vibrate with the force of the order, "or face my wrath."

I was unceremoniously jerked to my feet. Dozens of vampires bowed their heads, a few snuck glances at me. Bending over, I had to place my hands on my knees to support myself, my clothes hanging in tatters. Blood seeped from dozens of wounds, and a fresh wave of nausea rolled through me.

Ghost burst through the gathered crowd, whining and licking my face. "I'm all right," I told her. What a lie. Still in her giant psychopomp form, she was able to steady me when I pushed myself to standing.

A female in black leather from head to foot stepped forward. "We feared you were dead, Master."

Master? I pivoted to follow her gaze and arched a brow when I realized she was speaking to Killion. He was only slightly tousled, his dark hair mussed and jacket askew. If it weren't for the blood staining his expensive threads, no one would guess he'd been comatose only moments ago. He met my eyes. "I nearly was, Simone," he replied. " The weapon hit my heart, but Chloe saved me from permanent death."

A hushed murmur spread through the crowd, more gazes flicking to me and lingering as if taking my measure. Retracting their beastly forms, they appeared human now, but the vibe coming off them en masse continued to be animalistic. I didn't trust my voice, but I managed to raise a hand and croak out, "Hey."

Hey? Yep, that was the best I could manage at the moment.

Killion picked up the cross, slick with his blood. I glanced at my hands and shivered. That same liquid was all over me. In one swift movement, he brought the center of the cross down across his knee, snapping it in half. "You will treat her with the utmost respect. She is not to be harmed.

She is to be protected." He gave me a slight bow, tossing the pieces aside. "I am in your debt."

All heads mimicked his as another ripple of low voices sounded around me. Simone caught my eye for a long, drawn out moment, and her upper lip quivered, revealing the tip of a fang. As though compelled, she eventually tipped her chin down and turned her eyes to the floor.

I stumbled to a chair outfitted with straps and wires and hooked to a machine. "Thanks, I think. I, uh..." I glanced up to find Killion's steady gaze on me. "What just happened? Who was that?"

He surveyed the ruins of the statue, the two bodies. His features were pensive, but I could see the muscles in his body were tight with anger. "I believe that was our rogue."

I knew it. "He tried to kill you." I waved half-heartedly in the direction of Eye Patch and Mustache. "He silenced them so they wouldn't divulge his identity."

The vampire moved to my side, his followers shifting back in deference. "Correction, he attempted to kill *you*. I prevented that."

By throwing himself in front of the airborne object. My stomach twisted. "Then I owe you *my* thanks and you owe me an explanation, *Master*."

He must have seen the suspicion in my eyes, or maybe he read my mind—scary thought that. Either way, it seemed to amuse him. "Let's see to your wounds first."

The door burst open and Katarina ran in. She clapped and the sconces sprang to life all up and down the room. Really? They were on clappers? If only I'd known earlier, although I doubted they would have worked during the blackout. Her pets were with her, and they looked just as fearsome in the shadows of the illuminated room as they had outside. I wondered how she'd resurrected the one

Ghost had attacked. Were they vampire dogs? Zombies? "We tried to track them, but"—she punched the wall—"whatever magic he has, it's powerful."

Ghost pressed against my leg and panted. Something was on the end of her tongue. "What did you get into?" I grumbled, removing the saliva soaked item.

The tiny strip of black material felt familiar under my fingertips. I held it up in the light as Killion thanked Katarina.

"We'll need to reinforce this place," he told her. "He should've never been able to breach it, regardless of any powers."

She bowed her head. "I let you down. I deserve whatever punishment you see fit, Master."

Forcing myself to stand against my body's complaints, I held up the material for all to see. "How about you help me hunt down the rogue grim instead?"

Katarina's gaze came up, and so did the other female, who had been refusing to look at me at all. They both glanced at Killion, as he took the piece from my grip.

For a moment, no one said anything, and then he raised it above his head to show them. "Bring me this grim," he boomed out, and dozens of noses twitched, as if catching the scent. "I want his head."

THIRTY

Killion's limo slid to a stop in front of the church's courtyard. The driver held open the door, his scowl a thundercloud ready to break.

Katarina watched with a similar expression from the top step as I slid in without complaint and sunk into the cushy leather upholstery with a sigh. The interior was spacious with two leather seats facing each other. Soft lighting came from running lights along the door thresholds and a moon roof over our heads. Each door contained half a dozen controls and there was a divider in place between us and the driver.

I dropped my bag on the floor and Ghost jumped in my lap. Closing my eyes, I stroked her fur and ignored my ringing phone. The seat compressed as Killion joined me, and in seconds, we were off.

I was so wrung out, my mouth didn't want to form words. "When were you going to mention you're head of a bunch of vampires?"

"I apologize for their rudeness." His voice was butter soft. "They assumed you were my assailant, not my savior."

Which didn't answer my question. Maybe I should've figured it out—he was old and came from a royal family of the Undead, if my guess was correct. Death had labeled him an elder. The only kind I was familiar with were those from church, and I hadn't been in one of those since my parents' funeral, until tonight. "Is there some kind of bat signal that calls them when you're dying—or dying again, I guess?"

He chuckled and the sound warmed my insides and sent a shiver down my spine. "They are all connected to me, much like you are, only more intensely. We are family. They feel my pain."

Ghost licked my chin and I opened my eyes. Hers were staring at my face, concern in them. I scratched her ears. "I'm okay," I told her. She wagged her tail and settled, turning a couple times in my lap before lying down. "How did the reaper get in?"

He handed me a shot glass with amber colored liquor. That's when I noticed the mini-bar between us and the other seat. Had that been there when I'd climbed in?

"The statue has a secret compartment in which the church hid spies and others hunted by outside forces during medieval times. He somehow got past Katarina's watchful eye and must have been in there. He used some form of spell to cause the explosion."

I sipped the drink, the alcohol causing its own type of explosion in my mouth. It burned down my throat and I coughed several times. "Why does he want to kill me?" I croaked.

Killion turned to stare straight ahead at the screen divider. "Because you are dangerous."

"Me?" I scoffed. "You're the vampire master. You're the one who's been on his trail. I'm betting it was revenge for what I did to the others." I sat up, slightly disturbing Ghost.

"Wait. Are you a legit detective for Soul Management Group or did you lie about that, too?"

He flicked a glance my way, eyes glittering in the moonlight as we glided through town. "I have never lied to you."

"By omission you have." I sunk back again. "Are you or are you not a detective?"

"I have been with SMG for a hundred years." He pivoted in the seat to fully face me. "I will not lie to you, Chloe, ever."

His voice did that thing again, sending an excited shiver down my spine. I took another sip of the liquid courage. "How could I be more dangerous than you?"

"You've killed two of his men already, one a bonafide reaper. You aren't a supernatural and you've had no training." He touched a deep gouge on my arm that was healing slower than the others. "You are an unknown, an outlier, and that's always dangerous to those in power."

I swallowed hard, fighting the dueling urges to jerk away and at the same time, relish his gentle touch. His violet gaze held mine, depths of intriguing offers dancing in them.

...you are safe from my advances.

Was I? My phone buzzed. I startled, but he didn't so much as blink. Ghost lifted her head.

"What time is it?" I handed Killion the glass and dug out my cell. I had to wipe blood from the screen. The notifications said I'd missed multiple texts and a call from Nita, and I swore under my breath as I started to answer this time.

Killion stayed my hand, his surprisingly warm on my skin. "Perhaps you should clean up and rest before speaking to anyone."

While my injuries were healing, my clothes were still in shreds. I needed a shower, food, and sleep.

I needed a damn hug.

An image of me curling into Killion's strong chest and falling asleep flashed through my mind. Parts of my anatomy went crazy. Forcing that and his hand away, I pasted on a smile and answered the blaring device. "Don't be mad. I'm sorry I'm late for our study session. I lost track of time and I need to shower. Then I'll be over, okay?"

There was a long pause. "Chloe, you're scaring me for real. This is so unlike you. What is going on? Is it drugs? I can get you help. Is it Killion? Is he playing some sick game with you?"

I glanced his direction, knowing he could hear every word. A corner of his mouth was quirked and I narrowed my eyes at him. "It's not drugs and it's not Killion. I'm on my way home now. Want me to pick up Thai?"

"I already did." Her tone reminded me how she hated cold food. "Hurry up and get here. I'm at your place. And after your shower? We're having a long chat, Morticia."

She hung up. I slumped into the seat. "How am I going to explain this?" I pointed at my clothes.

Killion leaned forward, reaching under my legs. "I have something I believe will fit you perfectly."

I stared at his head, nearly in my lap with Ghost, and checked my desire to stroke his hair. He opened a hidden cabinet under the seat and withdrew a stack of folded garments.

I scooted Ghost onto the leather between us and took them. The shirt was a soft silk and when I held it up it rippled, the wrinkles falling out of it. The jeans were just as soft and had several well placed rips with metal accessories to give them a modern, hip look. Both were in my size.

"We are nearly to your apartment. You may change here in the car." He shifted so his back was to me, his attention on the night outside the window.

Right, like I was gonna strip to my undies, also tattered, with him sitting next to me. "How did you know my size?"

"I guessed."

"Good guess." He'd probably had plenty of girlfriends in a variety of shapes and sizes. These still had the tags on and I about dropped the shirt when I saw the price. "Dude."

He did that mind reading thing again. "You have nothing to fear, Chloe, and it's a skill I have—knowing women's bodies well enough to guess their size in clothing."

"That's creepy, and doesn't make me feel better."

He glanced back. "You will always be safe with me. I give you my vow."

My insides warmed, my spine going liquid. I wanted to sink into his words, his eyes. The screen shielded me from the driver, and the car windows were tinted. The sidewalks at this time of the late evening were mostly empty.

I looked at Ghost, sleeping away again and snoring, and knew she wouldn't accept the vampire if she didn't trust him, so why didn't I?

"You may feel the urge to tell your friend the truth," Killion said conversationally, "but I advise against it."

"Why, because she'll have me committed?"

"Because SMG does not take these things lightly. Your status as a grim must remain a secret from your human companions. It's stated in the manual. If you break that rule, they'll send Death after her."

I hadn't thought about him in hours. At least I had information to share—Killion wasn't the rogue leader. I also had an actual clue that could help us find the real one. "Will your servants find the rogue?"

"They aren't servants." He was offended.

"Fine, whatever. Will they sniff his trail, uncover his hangout?"

He drank the last of his liquor, then downed mine. "They enjoy heightened senses, but they are not bloodhounds. We shall see if any can ferret him out."

"So, *maybe* is the best you've got."

A shoulder moved in a shrug and he looked out the window once more. "We will find him, one way or another."

I snapped off the price tag on the silk shirt and then removed my wrecked one, deciding it wasn't hiding much anyway. The fabric whispered on my skin, and whatever magic it was imbued with erased the dried blood. "Amazing," I murmured.

Ghost yawned and stretched, and I bit my lower lip considering whether or not to change my pants. The knees were torn, the seams flayed open in spots. I could pass it off as a fashion statement gone wrong, if not for the blood, especially the large patch on my right thigh. "Good thing they didn't nick my artery," I muttered to myself.

The limo slowed and turned the corner onto my street. It was now or never. Shimmying out of the ruined pants, I wondered what to tell Nita. At least if I didn't look like I'd been attacked by rabid animals, I wouldn't have to explain that. As I slid a leg into the clean jeans, I noticed Killion stiffen. His profile was barely visible, but I saw his nostrils flare.

"Eww, are you...sniffing me?"

His hands tightened on the empty glasses, but he said nothing as the car edged to the curb in front of the apartment building. The front door flew open and Vera and Nita stepped out, both glaring.

Great. "Show time." I gathered up my bag.

The driver put the limo in park, but before he could jump out and open my door, Killion said, "Stay, Moss. I'll do it."

"I've got it." I reached for the handle. "I need to go to the morgue and see if I can talk to the ghosts of that couple who were killed by the rogues. As soon as I can get Nita to go home, that's where I'm headed."

I expected him to argue, or at least inquire why, but all he did was nod. "Shall I wait?"

Opening the door, I shook my head. Ghost jumped down to the street and I left the bloodstained clothes behind. "I'll text you when I'm ready."

On the sidewalk, I paused, knowing my audience was watching closely. I blew him a fake kiss as the limo pulled away.

"I knew it." Nita marched down the steps. "He *is* your boyfriend."

Ghost ran for Vera and I lifted my palms, offering a coy smile. If there was a way to excuse my newly erratic behavior, this was it. All I had to do was convince her I was in love. "Busted," I said, seeing the instant relief on their faces. "See? There's nothing to worry about."

Vera clapped and Nita poked me when I hit the steps. "He's a millionaire, isn't he?"

I had no idea. "Very eccentric," I explained. "We're keeping our relationship private, so I'd appreciate you both keeping mum about it, okay? I like him, but I don't know where it's going yet. Probably nowhere." It wasn't a lie. "Let's keep it between us."

They beamed, sucking me into the house, dozens of questions pouring from their mouths.

I answered a few, staying as vague as I could. "Seriously, it's no big deal," I insisted, checking the quiet street from the downstairs bay window. I looped an arm through Nita's, leading her up to my place. "And we have an anatomy test to study for."

She pinched my side. "You're not getting off that easily."

Vera called after us about making tea, and I told her that would be lovely.

At the top of the stairs, I let us in and Nita threw herself on the sofa. "I want all the details. Now."

Lies of omission came in handy over the next hour, and my gut cramped because of it. She was my best friend and I hated not being able to tell her the truth, but what was I supposed to say? It was for her own good, I told myself. I had to keep her safe.

THIRTY-ONE

By the time she was ready to leave, it was after midnight. "I'm going to flunk," she complained on my back porch. "You know this stuff inside and out. I wish I had your brain."

"You're not going to flunk," I reassured her, although she spent most of our study time asking about Killion and daydreaming about all of the things I'd get to do as his girlfriend. I told her he was a detective for a covert agency, which wasn't far from the truth. She'd wanted to know how we'd met, so I stuck close to reality on that as well, claiming I'd ran into him searching for Miss Pickles.

She hefted her backpack higher on her shoulder, yawning. "Do you work tomorrow?"

I honestly didn't know. "I've been so busy, I haven't checked the schedule." I mimicked her yawn. "I hope not. I could use the time to sleep in."

This caused her to wink and grin, assuming Killion was the cause. "Must be rough."

I swatted her leg. "Let's meet at the library at three and we'll study again before class, okay?"

She hugged me. "You're the best. See you then."

I watched her jog down the steps and round the corner to get to her car. I waved as she drove away, then took Ghost to do her duty. While she sniffed at the various plants and trees, I did a search on vampires. An interesting tidbit caught my eye—'Dracul,' as in Dracula, translated to dragon. Hmm. As with all old myths and legends, there was conflicting information. It was a rabbit hole best saved for another time. Besides, the little I read scared me, and being afraid wasn't going to help me, or anyone else.

Once we were back inside, I dumped out my bag. The blade was clean, not a drop of blood on it, but I wiped it off anyway. The echo of Eye Patch and Mustache's screams rang in my head.

How dare that reaper use *my* weapon to kill those two. How dare he attempt to kill me. Why hadn't he swung at me first? That was the thing that had been bugging me over the last two hours. Why would he kill his minions rather than let them go? The three of them could have ambushed me and Killion, eliminating both of us.

"How could you let him use you?" I questioned the scythe. "Traitor."

A humming came from it and the robes trembled.

I shoved both into the bag once more. Ghost watched, gnawing on her toy.

"Don't tell me you couldn't help it." I removed the heavy manual, zipped up the bag, and hefted the strap onto my shoulder. "If you're mine, you better not cheat on me with another grim."

Ghost barked, adding her two cents, and I ruffled her ears. She wagged and ran for the door.

Longingly, I looked at my bed as I passed, absentmindedly wondering if I should email SMG and update them about what had occurred. Or was that Killion's job? He'd worked for them for a hundred years—it boggled my mind. I'd have to ask about that later, but first, I had two ghosts to interview.

By the time we rounded the corner to hit the sidewalk, the limo sat waiting for me, Killion leaning against the side.

"I didn't send for you yet," I uttered just above a whisper in a mocking Killion-esque tone.

Ghost ran to him, dancing on her back legs to get him to pick her up.

He seemed to like the dog and cradled her against him. "There was no need."

I drew closer, fighting the urge to lick my lips. He'd changed into black jeans, a sweater, and a leather jacket. Even without the suit, he commanded authority and oozed sexiness. "You *are* psychic, aren't you?"

The corner of his mouth twitched, whether from Ghost's kisses or my question, I couldn't tell. "Your thought process is jumbled, yet uncomplicated. There's no need for me to read your mind."

Uncomplicated? I bristled, then shrugged. He wasn't exactly wrong. "In other words, you were watching the house."

"On the contrary." He opened the door and placed the dog inside on the seat. "I could feel your energy change when your friend left. I knew you were ready."

"My energy." Right. He could feel it because he'd given me his blood and brought me back to life. "That's not disturbing at all."

He motioned me in and I relented. How far my world had come since Friday night.

"Do you know how to call up a spirit?" I asked, once we

were moving. "Like a séance, I guess? Do we need candles and a crystal ball or something?"

If he found my ignorance entertaining, he didn't show it this time. I appreciated that. "You shouldn't need to call them if they are shades. They'll stay close to their bodies as much as possible."

I still didn't quite understand the term. Instead of reinforcing my novice status and asking Killion to explain, I drew out my phone and did a search. While the thirty thousand plus hits seemed to have similarities, there were also plenty of differences regarding the definition and scope of what a shade could and couldn't do. To my disappointment, there were just as many ways to dispense of them.

Ghost laid in Killion's lap. He glanced at the phone. "You were able to see Talon, and the magic at the church. You'll be able to see these spirits, as well."

"I didn't know what I was doing before."

"Exactly, and that's why it came easy to you, because you didn't overthink it. You simply let it happen."

My gaze went to the liquor cabinet. Maybe I needed a shot of something amber colored again. "What about other ghosts? Not the ones still semi-attached to their bodies like shades."

His eyes met mine and I felt him guess at the motivation behind my question. "When you died, you saw your mother, but that was a different frequency." Yep, he'd guessed correctly. "Your soul's matched hers at that point. This isn't the same. You must use your invisible senses to see, hear, and speak with shades, but you are still human. If you were to stay in their frequency for too long, it would leave you blind, deaf, or mute. Grave sight is not to be played with. Even those of us who have magic and walk between worlds do not linger in Death's."

Grave sight, another term I was unfamiliar with, but I got the gist. "There are spirits all around us, aren't there? I just can't see them because I'm not looking for them."

"It would be ill advised for you to seek your parents' on a regular or lengthy basis. You understand?" His tone was patient, gentle. It surprised me a little.

I sighed, disappointed. "Yeah, I get it."

A few minutes later, we slid into a parking spot in the rear lot of the hospital. I really wished I'd had a shot of that liquor, but it was too late now. Girding myself for what was to come, I grabbed the handle of my bag. "Let's go talk to some ghosts."

THIRTY-TWO

Dwayne was missing from the check-in area, meaning there were no bodies to be autopsied tonight. That made everything easier.

We skirted the desk and hustled down the hallway, me flipping on a few lights as we went. My mind was on the spirits—the shades—of our couple, and I nearly jumped out of my boots when the door to the makeshift kitchen swung open and Mary Lynn crashed into me. I toppled to the side and ran into Killion, but I bounced back.

"Chloe!" Mary Lynn clutched at her chest, eyes darting around. "I didn't expect you to be here."

She was dressed in a black turtleneck and jeans, a cute bolero jacket on top that had a skeleton pin on the breast pocket.

"I came in to catch up on paperwork." The lie rolled off my tongue with ease. "Seems like there's always more."

"People just keep dying, don't they?" She grinned. "What can you do, right?"

I chuckled. "Exactly."

She scratched Ghost under the chin and cooed at her. "Are you keeping your mommy company?"

The puppy barked and Mary Lynn drew her hand back. "Feisty tonight."

She didn't so much as glance in Killion's direction, so I didn't need to come up with an excuse for him being there. He was doing his disappearing act again, and luckily, she couldn't see him. "I hope you're not like me, wasting your Sunday night here."

She glanced at her watch. Her fingers shook slightly, twisting it around on her wrist. "Heading home from a friend's. I couldn't remember if I left my egg salad sandwich from Friday night in the fridge. You know how your uncle hates when it stinks things up. Say..." She scanned my face. "Are you okay?"

I tried to keep my features expressionless. "Sure, why?"

She stared into my eyes. "I don't know, you look...different."

Well that was ambiguous. "Being a college student can do that to you." I shrugged. "I've been studying for a big test. Late nights, you know."

That seemed to mollify her. She held up a fist. "If you need anything, I'm here for you."

I really needed to figure out why everyone kept thinking they needed to take care of me. I bumped hers with mine. "Will you take my anatomy test for me?" I joked.

She smiled and checked her watch a second time. Fiddled with her collar. "Gotta run. My date's waiting for me."

This surprised me. Her last romance had been a nightmare and she'd sworn off dating. "Seeing someone new?"

"We met at the hospital a few days ago, and I feel this connection, you know? This is so much deeper than any of those jerks from the app service. Seriously, she's amazing. We're doing the Thirteen Brew Scavenger Hunt downtown."

From the hospital. That could be anyone. "Do I know her?"

"I doubt it. She's a grief counselor and was here visiting a patient when we ran into each other. It was fate!"

Her enthusiasm seemed great, except it didn't quite reach her eyes. She was still burned from that last relationship, I guessed. "I thought the bars were closed on Sundays."

She went around me and headed for the entrance. "It's after midnight, silly, so technically it's Monday morning, and our first stop is the Dancing Cat for the Walking Dead whiskey. You should come!"

The yearly Halloween pub crawl was a tradition my generation looked forward to, but I wasn't one of them. "I appreciate the invitation, but when I'm done here, I have a soft bed begging for attention."

Since she always worked nights, this was her daytime. She waved over her shoulder. "Good luck with that exam."

As soon as I heard the door shut, I breathed a sigh of relief.

"Odd," Killion said. He was once more visible at my side.

"What is?"

"She didn't have any sandwich or bag containing one."

"Probably threw it out. It's not like egg salad keeps, and I doubt she wanted to bring it with her on a date."

He turned for The Pit and the coolers where the bodies were stored. "She lied to you. She is up to something."

Marching behind him, I rolled my eyes at the back of his head. "So you have a built in lie detector?"

"I saw that," he said. "Humans have certain tells. She exhibited several."

Badging us in, I made a mental note to learn those, but at the moment, I had more pressing matters to focus on. I dug into my bag and removed a lighter. I'd scanned a quick internet article about seances. The person leading it usually lit a candle. "Here, stand over there and hold this."

He looked at the cheap thing with some disgust. "Whatever for?"

"We don't have candles, so we have to make do."

His brows rose ever so slightly. "You don't need them to call the dead, but I do advise you to focus."

I rubbed my hands together. "Focus is my middle name, and the lighter flame will help." I checked the computer to see which cold boxes the couple were in. Number nine held the woman, and I opened that door first. The aroma of the chilled corpse wafted out, and I held my breath, tugging the metal tray with her on it from the cooler.

Her face under the sheet was a pale and sickly gray. My stomach felt squishy and odd. I kept thinking her eyes would twitch or her chest might rise and fall. "Flick your Bic," I told the vamp.

"Excuse me?"

It was an old commercial, and I'd assumed he'd heard the phrase. "Never mind. Just light it. Like you said, I need to focus."

"We don't want to trigger the fire suppression system," he pointed out, glancing up at the sprinklers overhead.

"Trust me, that little flame won't."

The corners of his eyes narrowed. "You have experimented with lighting up in here?"

"Unfortunately, nothing so fun. I've had in-depth, boring training on every system and what is allowed and prohibited in this area. While we're breaking a rule about open flames, this won't cause any harm."

"It would be better—"

I held up a hand. "Let me do my thing. Please," I added. I wasn't angry, but my nerves were shot. His cool expression let me know he didn't appreciate it. "Sorry, I'm just—"

"I know," he said, the lighter flicking on. "I simply don't want you calling in more ghosts than intended."

"There are only two shades, right?" I motioned at the poor woman. "We're fine."

Staring at the flame, I took a deep breath and mentally reached out to the deceased with my mind, reciting her name over and over again. "Here goes nothing."

THIRTY-THREE

I was wrong about Mr. and Mrs. Jensen being the only shades.

Killion made a noise, and a frosty air enveloped me. I'd been so focused on the flame, I'd blocked everything else out, letting my vision blur. The world snapped back into place with the noise, and I jumped, nearly tripping over Ghost.

Around me, five spectral figures shimmered in the air. Not one looked happy to see me, and I certainly wasn't thrilled about them either. Especially since none were the Jensens and two were the men from the nave—Eye Patch and Mustache.

"Not good," I said. "What do I do?"

All of the gray apparitions opened their mouths in unison. The high-pitched screech we'd heard earlier in the church filled the room. I clapped my hands over my ears and Killion did the same, dropping the lighter.

"I'm sorry," I tried to shout over the noise. "I didn't mean to call any of you!"

They floated toward me, closing in, their mouths

moving. My palm itched and Ghost grew in front of my eyes.

"Send them..." Killion yelled to me, but I couldn't hear the rest above the commotion.

"Where?"

"Focus!"

I didn't so much hear him say it, but saw his lips form the word. "I'm trying!"

Realizing I might be able to continue my interrogation of Eye Patch and Mustache, I reigned in my fear as they reached for me.

The scythe flew through the air. As though I had no control, my hand shot out and closed around the handle. Ghost jumped in front of me, snarling, and like it had previously, the blade took over. It swung in a circle.

The instant it touched each ghost, they vanished.

Expecting the rush I'd felt when I'd harvested Talon, I was disappointed when nothing happened. I dropped the blade, the metal clanging on the concrete floor. Bending at the waist, I braced my hands on my knees and gulped air. I didn't know if they could have hurt me, but their intent to try had blazed in their eyes. "Holy dead people," I said. "What just happened?"

Killion retrieved the lighter and Ghost licked my face. "You called the shades and they came. At least we know you can do it."

"I called Mrs. Jensen, not those"—I waggled a finger in the air—"things. And I blew my chance to get more out of Eye Patch and his cohort. Now they're gone and I could've found out what they knew." I stood and kicked at the lowest row of coolers.

Killion returned the blade to my bag. "They'll be back."

I eyed him. "How do you know?"

"You chased them off, but you didn't get their souls to cross over."

I huffed and looked at the unmoving body on the table. "Why didn't the Jensens appear?"

He studied her, too. "Unknown. If they were killed by a human, even one with power like our grim imposters, perhaps their souls aren't stuck here."

I could hope that for them. Having it tethered to a dead body wasn't a picnic. My ears were still ringing, and I tried to pop them. "That noise they made—it was the same one we heard in the church."

He met my eyes, and I could see he wanted to reach out to me. He held back. "Those killed by our rogue grim are under his control and he's keeping them mute, so they can't tell anyone who he is."

The bastard had outsmarted us again. "I'm sorry," I said to Mrs. Jensen. "I hope I didn't disturb you." To Killion, I asked, "Should I try with her husband?"

"I suggest we regroup for now."

I liked that idea. I returned her to the cooler. Ghost shifted back to her puppy size, and I picked her up, accepting my bag from Killion. As we departed The Pit, I turned off the lights and locked up. Outside on the sidewalk, I took a deep breath of fresh air. "I stink at this job."

"It was a good idea," he told me. "The execution was weak."

Moss pulled up in the limo. "You have a way with backhanded compliments, you know that?"

Killion opened the rear door and I got in and scooted across the leather seat. "I state facts."

That much was true. Through the windshield, I noticed a sleek black Porsche leaving the lot. It was an older model, but appeared to be in excellent shape. As it took off down the street, I saw a woman in the passenger seat whose profile looked like Mary Lynn.

At least someone was having fun. I wasn't sure I ever would again. Slumping low in the seat, I blew a raspberry. Ghost cocked her head at the noise and decided it was playtime. She jumped at my face, growled, then licked me and hopped back, nearly tumbling from my lap. Killion and I both reached for her at the same time and our hands collided.

He hung onto mine and that sizzle his stare always produced in certain areas of my body exploded. It felt like the hair on my head would combust and a strange electricity shot down my spine.

"You've had a rough weekend," he said gently, the words rolling off his tongue. "I am concerned for your safety. I would feel better if you allowed me to take you to a safe house where you can rest and be protected by my security."

Those eyes, that voice. He was mesmerizing. Everything in me wanted to say, "I'm all yours." Luckily, I still had a few brain cells working and wondered, was it really me thinking that or was he enchanting me somehow?

As he continued to hold my hand, I didn't pull away. I'd been on my own for a while, and I'd been struggling to hold it together. Trying to take classes, pay bills, and hold down two jobs—I was literally exhausted, mentally and physically. No wonder everyone wanted to help me.

On top of all that, I was now a grim. I couldn't tell anyone, not even my best friend. I sort of sucked at it, too, and this rogue dude was sending his minions after me. He might have succeeded if it hadn't been for the man— vampire—next to me.

Vampires—I shivered at the thought. The icy hatred in their eyes, the way their claws had ripped into my skin.

Killion seemed to register the tug of war going on in my mind. He released my hand gently. "I give you my word, no harm will befall you, if you come home with me."

I shifted slightly away and hugged Ghost, staring out at the passing scenery. Neither of my options—go home and worry all night about the rogue grims paying me a visit, or accept Killion's offer and worry about vampires ripping me to shreds—was appealing. "I can't."

There was a long, pregnant pause. Ghost wiggled from my arms. She hopped over to his lap and he stroked her fur. "May I suggest a compromise?"

I glanced at him and a spark of hope filled my chest. "I'm listening."

"There is a place you will be safe and I will not worry about you." He touched the intercom button on the divider. "Moss, change of plans. Take us to The Beaumont."

The driver responded and the car took a turn. "Yes, sir."

"What's that?"

"You've never heard of The Beaumont Hotel?"

I sat up straight. The place that hosted the rich and famous around town? "You're kidding, right?"

He shook his head.

A luxury hotel? Who could beat that? There was just one problem. "That place is haunted!"

THIRTY-FOUR

"You can practice calling shades," he replied. "After a rest."

"No way." I shook my head. "The only ghosts I want to talk to right now are under some gag order from our rogue. I don't want to practice with others."

The limo glided smoothly through the night and Killion patted my arm. "You can't go home right now, it's too dangerous. You need sleep and sustenance."

I needed a new life. "I'll crash with Nita, or my aunt and uncle."

"You wish to put them in danger?"

Of course I didn't. Desperation made my stomach churn. "But...a haunted hotel?"

"The room you'll be in will be ghoul-free," he assured me.

His eyes in the shadowy backseat were like melted chocolate. The edges of his irises had darkened to a deep purple. I could feel my blood responding to whatever he was trying to get me to do. "You better not be doing that compulsion thing on me."

One brow lifted. "Compulsion *thing?*"

"I read books. I've seen movies. I know vampires can manipulate us *mere* humans. Put us under a thrall. I've also seen you create glamours."

His lips twitched. "You are no mere human, and I would never cross that boundary with you."

Either I was tired or he was lying. It didn't matter, I did need sleep and food. Also a shower. And those eyes...they were sending me into overdrive. Purple has always been my favorite color. "Fine, but I don't want to practice calling shades, or ghosts, or anything other than a long, hot shower. Not until I feel I have a better handle on this ability."

He held out a hand. "Deal."

At least he wasn't asking for a blood contract. Reluctantly, I shook, shivering when a tingle ran up my arm and across my chest. It seemed to stop at my scythe tattoo. Our eyes locked and we stayed that way, holding hands for several deceptively slow beats of my heart. "Deal," I finally said, my voice rough and breathy.

"We're here, master," the driver's voice over the speaker interrupted us. I pulled my hand back, slipping it between my knees.

The limo crawled to a stop and a bellman, in a burgundy and gold suit, stepped from the hotel's grand entrance to open the back door for us. "Welcome home, Mr. Reveux."

Ghost started to jump out. I caught her before she could. "Wait, what?!"

Killion reached for my hand and winked. "Good evening, Charles. Is the penthouse ready?"

As I stepped out into the night air, the bellman bowed. "As always, sir." I caught myself gawking yet again, when he inclined his hand toward my bag. "Would you like me to bring that up for you?"

"No." I clutched it tighter. "Thank you, I'll carry it."

He dipped his head. "Very good."

Killion's hand touched my lower back as he guided me through the glass and gold doors. "This way."

"You own this place?" Ghost wiggled in my arms, wanting down to sniff at the antique furniture and intricate wool rugs.

Several staff members greeted us, including a woman at the front desk. She was model perfect, beautiful heart shaped face with dark eyes that tilted up at the corners. "Mr. Reveux, always a pleasure. The wardrobe you ordered earlier has been sent up. Shall I ring the butler to prepare the usual?"

"Thank you, Oki, that would be appreciated." He led me down a white marbled hall with a glass dome ceiling. Giant plants, more antiques, and gilded paintings assaulted my eyes everywhere I looked. No ghosts, though, which was a relief. There was a dragon motif—classy and understated—with statues you'd normally see in a museum watching as we passed them. The elevators sported a gothic flare like the rest of the first floor.

"Nice digs." I tried not to gawk like the destitute nerd I was.

"I built the place in 1901."

"Modeled on that castle in Transylvania?"

If he was offended—or humored—by the question, he didn't show it. He guided me inside the glass elevator. "You don't care for dragons?"

There it was again. "Are you serious?"

His mouth quirked so briefly, I might have missed it if I hadn't had my gaze pinned on his face. He placed his thumb on a scanner at the top of the button stack. The doors closed with a melodic whisper. It sounded so lifelike, I glanced around to be sure we were alone. "You are always filled with curiosity." He sounded amused. "Do you wish to know if they are real, too?"

My eyes went wide. "Dragons are real? No way! Now I know you're joking."

This got a chuckle. "At one time, they existed. They were hunted to extinction long before my birth, but I would have enjoyed tangling with them."

"Tangling?" I snorted and leaned back against the wall, sorry they weren't around anymore, but also a tad relieved. Could you imagine if they were? "My Aunt Camille loves dragons. She has dozens of sculptures in her herb garden. Wish I could tell her they aren't a myth."

"*Fiecare mit are o semints de adevăr.* Every myth has seeds of a truth."

Just like vampires? "You've had—*have*—quite the life."

He scratched Ghost under the chin and she went all dewy-eyed. "I enjoy life immensely."

"Killion Reveux. Sounds French."

"I adopted it when I came to America."

Ghost wiggled and flirted with him. "What's your real name?"

His violet eyes met mine. He was close enough to kiss. "You must earn the privilege of learning that."

My breath caught at the hint of challenge in his irises. "You're weird."

"Names have power, especially in the supernatural world. Only a select few have ever learned mine."

Challenge accepted. I would earn the right to know it, too. A new thought struck at the idea of who the "select few" might be, and I dropped my attention to the dog. "Do you bring all your, um, friends here? Girlfriends? Or men friends?" *Geez, Chloe.* I sounded the way I had after the accident, when I'd finally started speaking after two months of silence. I struggled to find correct terms or put words together that made a normal sentence. "Vampire peeps? Whatever you prefer?"

"What makes you think that?" His demeanor became less playful, yet he seemed continually entertained at my awkwardness. "And for the record, I have always preferred females, vampire or otherwise."

Otherwise, as in *human?* A fresh shiver, slow and tantalizing, tickled its way down my spine. "You have a penthouse suite ready and the manager is calling the butler to prepare 'the usual.' Sounds like you visit often."

"I rarely have free time, but when I do, this is my preferred home. However, I keep my name off the formal papers so the place is not linked to me. Only my nest know my connection to it, with the exception of a handful of others, such as yourself. You're safe here."

The staff were vampires. Oh goodie. *Better than ghosts.* Once again, the elevator made an almost human sigh as it stopped at the top floor. I continued to stare at him, refusing to move when he motioned me out.

He pressed a button to keep the doors open and leaned against the glass. Here, the view beyond it was encased in a black void. Only the LEDs over our heads and lining the floor lit the space. "What is it?"

"Is there anything else you haven't told me, your royal mentorship?"

He held my questioning gaze, unperturbed and bold as brass. "I assure you there are many. As I've stated, I'm three hundred years old. If you require a detailed history of who I am, where I've lived, and what I've done, we will be standing here a very long time."

"I don't like being blindsided or feeling like an idiot. Like I did at the church when I discovered you're a master vampire. Like I did when Death told me you were a vampire to begin with. I should have heard it from you, not someone else."

My distress seemed to surprise him. "I did not imagine such labels would matter, and as I've admitted, I am a private being. I do not share my personal history and facts with just anyone. You have my apologies." He beckoned once more to the penthouse door. "Shall we? If you feel unsafe at any time and prefer I take you somewhere else, I give you my word, I will do so. But at least consider showering and enjoying a meal."

Ghost glanced up at me. She was as hungry as I was. "Is Vera in any danger?"

"Unlikely, but I have stationed security around her house. My best people are watching over her."

I hadn't expected that. I would check in on her later. "Thank you. That relieves my mind."

Ghost barked and wagged her tail. Tomorrow, when I felt more like myself, maybe I'd have the energy to dive deeper into all of this. Legs heavy, I trudged into the penthouse, ready for that shower, and as much food as I could consume.

THIRTY-FIVE

The luxury space was bigger than ten of my apartments and a hundred times classier.

High-ceilings, plush carpeting, palatial windows, and more of those museum-quality statues greeted us. The air was redolent with the scent of magnolias and lemon, opulent vases filled with tasteful floral arrangements and various herb topiaries softening the masculine leather and stone.

The walls sported shades of gray and deep red. Ornate mahogany furniture, covered in spice tones, warmed the living room, and a fireplace with a built-in wall of bookshelves invited you to spend an evening of reading and pleasant conversation on a chilly night.

A view of the elite north side of town drew me to stare out the balcony doors, the nightscape scattered with city lights. The terrace ran the length of the building's side and was covered with luscious flowering plants and twinkling fairy lights that mimicked those of my town. "Is this heaven?" I muttered, running my fingers over an ivy covered railing. A hot tub bubbled away in the corner. "No, it's a vampire's lair," I finished, twisting the Field of Dreams' line.

Returning to the living area, I ran my fingers across the back of a burgundy sofa, noticing the tray ceiling and chandelier overhead. The upholstery was soft and velvety. A delicious new smell mixed with the others, suggesting food was being cooked. Craning my neck, I viewed a generous dining space with a table that could easily seat sixteen or more people.

Ghost jumped on a matching chair and I shooed her off, but Killion seemed unconcerned. "She won't hurt anything."

I bit my tongue before I blurted the laundry list of all the items she'd destroyed already.

He pointed to a hallway off to the right. "The master is down the hall with an en suite bath. You'll find clothing in the walk-in closet—I had my assistant acquire a few items in your size, but if you don't find anything that pleases you, I can order up what you prefer and have it here by morning. Help yourself."

"How did you know I would need them?"

"I like to be prepared." He walked to a wet bar on the wall between the living and dining areas. Various dark liquors gleamed in crystal decanters. "Would you care for a drink?"

At that moment, I would have consumed anything, and copious amounts of it, but getting drunk wasn't wise. "Water, please." I smelled of the morgue and this was all... too much. I desperately needed a moment to myself. "I'm just going to..." I hitched my thumb over my shoulder, and at his nod of understanding, I headed down the hall.

The opulent bedroom and bath combo was practically its own apartment. Cushy chairs waited expectantly in a reading area in front of another fireplace. A modern kitchenette, with marble countertop, wine cooler, and a high-end cappuccino machine was across from that. A second set of sliding glass doors opened on to the balcony.

In this space, there were heavy blackout shades and curtains. While they were open now, not a smidge of daylight could penetrate the space if they were drawn. The view was equally amazing, and I wished for time to stand outside and take it all in. Above the fireplace was a painting of a dog, a large, hairy beast of an animal with kind, wise eyes, that seemed to stare straight into my heart. He'd been painted in front of a fireplace, much like the one I stood before, and a gold plaque on the bottom of the frame read, "Beowulf." I would have to ask about him.

Peeking my head into the walk-in closet, I blinked several times at the organized, expensive designer wardrobe in one built-in section that would have made Carrie Bradshaw from Sex in the City fame, envious. Dante's Grove boasted a whopping twenty-thousand folks and only a handful of un-glamorous stores. We were no New York City, and I didn't have an obsession with shoes, yet I still felt as giddy as her character would at the selection on display.

What I needed, however, was something with less *wow*, and more soothing, with basic cotton softness to it. Searching for pants, it took a bit before I stumbled on a drawer filled with high-end yoga pants. Too good to exercise in, in my humble opinion, but super comfortable. I tried a couple pairs on and selected a shimmery black. The fabric molded to me like a second skin and I almost dropped into a down dog just for fun. Instead, I turned this way and that in front of a floor-to ceiling mirror and admired myself. *Must be magic.* I actually looked fit in them.

The antique fixtures in the bathroom sparkled under

the soft lighting, the marble shower and tub, decadent as the rest of the place. All I cared about was that the water was hot and the soap and shampoo cleaned off the night's ick, yet the hedonistic wealth of my mentor's lifestyle was fascinating. Letting the warmth of the shower soothe me, I soaped and rinsed three times, breathing in the luxurious scent of the shower gel, some mix of jasmine and roses, with a hint of cinnamon, and felt much better. I stayed long enough my skin became prune-y and my sore muscles relaxed.

Ghost was scratching at the door when I finished, and I let her in while I towel-dried my hair. She sniffed the entire space, and me, before padding back out.

In the bedroom, I found a tray with water in a crystal goblet and a shot of rich brown liquor. I sniffed the alcohol and caught the scent of butter. Bourbon. Really *good* bourbon. Not typically my drink of choice, but down the hatch it went, melting my throat and warming my chest. I followed it with a goblet's worth of the water, a cool compliment to the bourbon, then returned to the main area, following the heavenly scents of food.

A feast awaited me, Killion nursing his own drink at one end of the immense dining table. His eyes scanned me in the yoga pants and an oversized shirt that had come from his massive collection. It was a buttery yellow and felt like sin. It also smelled like him. He perused me again from head to toe, the reaction that passed across his face flitting by too quickly for me to define. It seemed to be a mixture of surprise and satisfaction.

He cleared his throat, blinked, and refocused his attention on his glass. "I was unsure how hungry you might be, but after witnessing your robust appetite early, I ordered one of everything."

My eyes bugged out and my stomach growled. The table was covered from one end to the other, with the most food I'd ever seen in my life. All kinds of dishes from varying cultures, most too fancy for my usual peanut-butter-and-jelly lexicon.

A butler stepped from a corner shadow and gave me a polite, if cool, nod. "May I offer a beverage? We have anything you desire."

My gaze returned to the selection of taco ingredients. "Just water," I told him, picking up an elegant china plate and attempting not to salivate. Along with filling several shells to their brims, I rounded out my selection with two pieces of pizza, a bowl of shrimp étouffée, and a side of pancakes. There was no way I'd be able to eat it all, but I was ravenous and I'd do my best.

The butler filled a new goblet and pulled out my chair. I sat and thanked him awkwardly. Then I startled when he snapped a burgundy colored napkin that matched the couch and drapes and started to tuck it into my lap for me. I grabbed his wrist. "I can handle it, thanks."

He glanced at Killion, who gave a nearly imperceptible nod, and then disappeared into the shadows once more.

It kind of freaked me out, but I was too hungry to give it much thought. Killion wasn't going to eat, by the looks of things, so I descended on the food with a vengeance. A moan escaped my lips at how good every single bite was. I didn't even care how messy the tacos were, or the fact my mentor watched with a bemused expression at my gusto.

Propriety tugged at me once I'd finished the tacos and a pizza slice. There were fancier choices, like lobster and steak, but those weren't the least appealing. I dug into the shrimp bowl, delighting in the tangy sauce the chef had used. "You know, I can't eat all of this." I waved a hand at the selection. "I feel guilty for wasting it."

"My butler is a chef who loves his job. The opportunity to put his skills on display is rare and he's happy to have someone who appreciates them. I'm afraid I'm not a foodie, although I do import my coffee beans and certain wines from France. Those are vices I afford myself. Don't worry about waste—the leftovers will be donated to the shelter on Second Street."

A vampire with a heart of gold. Someone should make a movie. "That's generous and it alleviates my guilt, so thank you." The possibility that he was simply keeping future potential human donors well-fed crossed my mind. I chose to believe that wasn't the case, and I wasn't ready to think about who he snacked on. He'd mentioned they were volunteers, so I'd accept that. Better to stay focused on our investigation. "We have a rogue, beyond Gustafson, who's running this ring of grim-wannabes. Those guys are pretending to be reapers and killing people in order to gain magic?"

Killion nodded at my simple synopsis, but stayed quiet while I devoured the bowl and bit into the second pizza slice. The cheese was still warm, which surprised me, and melted on my tongue. I chewed, swallowed, and continued to work through everything that had happened. "Said rogue tried to kill us first by sending the three goons this morning. Then again, by infiltrating the church, blowing up a statue, and managing to use a sacred religious artifact as a weapon. On an aside, talk about bad karma—blowing up Saint Ann? She was Jesus' grandmother. Bad move."

Another nod. "The one we seek is powerful and even more shrewd than I'd anticipated. I doubt he is worried about karma."

Speaking of power. "And you're a vampire master, who

happens to be the owner of the fanciest hotel in the tri-state area, and works for SMG."

"Why does my background bother you so much?"

I polished off the slice, thinking that over, and picked up the next one. "I've been thrown into a world I didn't know existed and I have trust issues, okay? Is there anything of importance you haven't told me? This is your chance to restore that trust."

His fingers rubbed the stem of his glass. A simple, yet sexy move. "I'm amazed at your capacity to consume food."

Frustration filled my already full stomach. "I'm serious, Killion. Stop trying to distract me, and answer my question."

He held my eyes, his violet ones warm and alluring. The crystals hanging from the chandelier dropped tiny rainbows across him. "I am, as well. Your uniqueness intrigues me."

We were at least six feet apart, and yet if felt as if he were stroking those strong fingers down my back, rather than the glass. Tugging my gaze away, I could barely swallow. My pulse skittered and I reached for my water.

Sensing my unease, he sighed softly. "I am unsure how to fulfill your request." The words were velvet against my skin. "As I barely know you, I'm not sure what you deem important."

The coolness of the liquid centered me. I choked down another swig and took a deep breath. Time to come at this with something easy for him. "Who's the dog?"

A brow arched in question.

"In the bedroom. The painting? Beowulf? Was he yours?"

An easy smile crossed his face. "An amazing animal. Watched over me growing up and helped me defeat many an enemy. He shed fiercely and my mother was beside herself with his, shall we say, intense odor, but I adored him."

I found myself smiling, too. "They touch our hearts in unexpected, but remarkable ways. What breed was he?"

"Carpathian Shepard mix."

Romanian, of course. "They are handsome dogs."

"He was special...unique." His eyes darkened as they met mine.

My heart gave a skip at the word, but it was that look that made my insides go gooey. He liked unique things.

I opened my mouth to say something sarcastic or change the direction of that intense attention on me, but was speechless. Awkwardly, I fed my face instead, dropping my own gaze to my plate.

This seemed to amuse him. "Any other personal questions? At some point, I will turn the tables so I may learn more about you."

I swallowed the too-big bite I'd shoved in my mouth. My cheeks heated like they were on fire. Once I could speak without being impolite, I decided it was time to get back to our investigation. "Your vampires haven't traced the scent of the robe to our rogue?"

His amusement vanished. "I spoke to Katarina a few minutes ago. They tracked him to the abandoned warehouse complex outside of town, but lost the scent there. That appears to be a dead end."

He'd said it was a long shot, but I felt deflated. "What about Ghost? Do you think she could track him?"

Hearing her name, the dog raised her head from the plush bed someone had placed in front of the fireplace. Killion stared at the liquid, swirling it while he thought it over. "She's not a bloodhound, but she has extraordinary abilities. May be worth a try."

Hope sparked again. I dug into the pancakes, delighted to see they had slivers of chocolate in them. Again, I almost moaned when the first piece hit my tongue. This wasn't just chocolate—it was heaven. A part of me wished I could simply sit here and pig out, totally enjoying the delicacies and not worrying about killers and monsters. Regrettably, I couldn't. I cut through the stack and swirled the chocolaty goodness in real maple syrup. "We need to explore every avenue, especially if the shades can't talk to me. Who do you think killed Susie and Lamar Jensen, if not the wannabes?"

"Perhaps, as you mentioned, they died of natural causes."

We couldn't rule it out. Contemplating that, I ate the last of the pancakes and shoved the plate away, thoroughly stuffed. I probably couldn't walk at this point and I tugged at the waistband of the yoga pants. My eyelids sagged, and I blinked several times, trying to dismiss the lethargy.

"You need rest." He rose and pulled out my chair. "Come."

The butler/chef appeared once more, inquiring if the food was acceptable. He seemed dismayed at the amount left over.

"It was delicious." I smiled at him. "The sauce on the shrimp was the best I've ever tasted."

He seemed pleased, yet when we passed him, he lowered his gaze, bowing his head, but not before I saw a flicker of distaste pass over his features.

I'd done nothing to these vampires. Why did they dislike me so much? Because I was human? A grim?

"Would you prefer I take you home?" Killion asked. "Or will you be my guest tonight?"

My stomach ached pleasantly and I rubbed it, feeling a food coma coming on. "I'll stay." I stifled a yawn. "I should feed the dog."

"She has been attended to," Killion assured me. He led me to the door of the bedroom. His hand brushed my arm. "Remember, you're safe. Sleep well."

He was close enough to kiss. I caught myself licking my lips. "You're not leaving, right? Your butler doesn't care for me."

"No member of my nest will harm you. Ever."

His nest. Was I now part of that, because I'd ingested his blood?

The conundrum was real. What I'd told him was true—after those two big reveals about who he was, I felt unsettled regarding our relationship. I felt it even more so with him so close and me about to sleep in his bed. No coffin, then? No grave dirt? "I still want to stay."

The corners of his mouth twitched with a repressed smile. "Very well, then. Good night, Chloe."

He walked away, me staring after him and praying I'd made the right call.

THIRTY-SIX

The past few days caught up to me and it was lights out before I could even climb under the covers.

At one point, I woke to find Ghost curled beside me and the light on the nightstand still on. I fumbled to turn it off and drew her closer, before succumbing to a deep sleep once more.

Mom and Dad took me to Yellowstone when I was nine. I dreamed about an open field with yellow flowers and mountains in the distance—a hologram of the memories I had of the park.

It's not my parents, but Killion who's standing next to me. "Lift the veil," he instructs.

I glance around. "What veil?"

He points to my left and I see the corner of a gray fabric, realizing that my view has the same shade of filter over it. The veil seems to breathe and ripple over the landscape, nearly invisible. "I don't want to," I tell him, pulling my hands into my belly.

"You must."

I swallow and fight the compulsion to do it, as everything in me recoils. "Please don't make me."

His voice is confident. "You're strong, Chloe, and I'm here. You can handle it."

With trembling fingers, I reach out to take the corner. It feels cold and slippery. The breeze tugs it from my grasp. Like a child trying to grab a paper on the wind, I lunge. Goosebumps trail up my arms when I snag it, hopscotching over my shoulders and down my back. The texture of it is like the material of the robes—death is woven into it.

While the sun shines over the field and the yellow flowers reach for its golden rays, my breath frosts the air. The joints of my fingers ache, the skin turning blue.

The fabric is like a band aid, covering a wound. Gritting my teeth to stop their chattering, I set my jaw and tighten my grip. With one jerk, I yank the filter away.

The faces of ghosts and other horrors surge toward me, the landscape bleached of color. The gray lifelessness is its own landscape, cold and unyielding.

The lost souls are like weights, stuck in what I imagine is some type of purgatory, as they cling to my energy. Claws scratch the air. Their faces contort into macabre masks.

The blood in my veins freezes, my heart stops. I can't breathe or move. "Help," I scream, but it's only a whisper in my mind.

"CHLOE, WAKE UP." The bed dipped, a hand landing on my leg. The two sensations jolted me from the nightmare.

Blinking the last remnants of it away, I sat straight up and swung my fist before my eyes were fully open. A strong hand closed around my wrist and stopped the punch.

Death grinned at me. "Nice hook."

I blinked again and scrambled away, jerking free from his hold. My heart raced, traces of the dream stuck to me like cobwebs. "How did you get in here?"

His big body shifted and Ghost's small one leaped into his lap. He gave her a pat. "I heard about what happened in the church." He laughed when she stood on her hind legs to lick his chin. "I wanted to make sure you were okay."

Surprised he would care, I rubbed sleep from my eyes. "The rogue tried to kill me. That's three attempts on my life since Friday night. I'm hardly okay."

He pinched my arm good-naturedly. "You're still alive."

"You suck at pep talks."

His hand was surprisingly warm and gentle as he began stroking my bare skin. "Tell me what happened."

I smacked his touch away and prodded him to move so I could swing my legs over the edge. "Killion isn't your guy," I told him after I gave him a quick rundown. Ghost hopped into my lap, sensing my distress, and it was my turn to receive puppy kisses. "The shades have some kind of gag spell on them. All they can do is make a horrible screeching noise like our rogue made at the church."

Death frowned. "That means the rogue is a tweener, like you."

"A what-er?"

His thigh nudged mine when he kicked his heels out and crossed his legs at the ankles. "Since you died and came back, you can move between worlds now. You walk in the liminal spaces, when you want to. Tweener is the—"

"Nickname. I get it." Something occurred to me. "But that means Avi was, too, right? Are the Undead all tween-ers? They've died and been resurrected." At least most had.

"Different situation entirely. They have defied the laws of nature, of life and death, of the universe, throwing things out of balance. Therefore, with the exception of an elite few, they are not able to walk in that dimension."

"Were you there when I died? You said we didn't get to officially meet then."

He pivoted his head to look directly at me. "I don't attend every death. In fact, I don't for most. I'd be running all over the place. But Gustafson's, like any grim's, jerked me there, especially since his contract wasn't up."

A chill swept over me. My fingers were still as cold as ice and I rubbed my hands together to warm them. "If our rogue is one of these tweeners, you can narrow down our suspect list, right?" Excitement took over, the thought gelling. "Not every grim has died and been resurrected, correct?" Ghost jumped down and barked, now excited, too. She was ready to play, or maybe she had to pee. With her, it was hard to tell. I stood. "That's it! That's how we can figure it out."

Death smiled at my enthusiasm. "It's worth checking into, but quite a few grims have experienced death. That's what makes them excel at their job."

"Oh." Defeated, I sunk back down beside him. "This sucks."

He patted my leg. "You've got him scared. All these months, Killion's been chasing and making no progress, but you come along and take out his top lieutenant, along with three of his followers. That's why he's bearing down on you."

"I only killed one follower. He decapitated the other two at the church to keep them from talking." It wasn't logical that he'd taken the time to kill them and not me. I said as much to Death. "Strategy is apparently not his forté."

"You're a formidable opponent, not an easy kill. He

planned for the cross to get the job done. When it didn't, he realized he'd have to go head-to-head with you, and that scared him off. He took out the others and ran when the vamps showed. I'd call that strategic."

"Killion nearly died for me. If I hadn't pulled that cross out..."

"But you did, and he's fine. Chloe, I know it appears he's your friend, but that whole thing doesn't add up. It could have been staged. You need to stay alert and be wary of him, okay?"

"It was not staged." Was he really that jaded against my mentor? "If you'd been there, you'd know that. Killion is not the rogue, so why won't you cut him some slack?"

He held up his hands in mock surrender. "He may not be the killer we're after, but that doesn't mean he's innocent."

I felt annoyance, possibly at myself for wanting to defend Killion, but mostly at Death for trying to make me feel incompetent again. "You just find out who the other tweeners are," I told him, opening the bedroom door to usher him out. "Let me worry about Killion."

Rubbing his palms on his jean-clad thighs, he rose and patted Ghost on the head. "Giving me orders now?"

The tone of his voice was light, but the look in his eyes was not. My legs instinctively quivered with the need to run. It was everything I could do to remain still and stare him down. "Help is a two way street. You want mine? I need yours."

One finger waggled at me. "You're tough. I like that. Killion's lucky to have you on his side." He moved close, forcing me to glance up in order to maintain eye contact. Then he pinched my chin gently and lowered his voice. "Just don't forget who you work for."

THIRTY-SEVEN

Death disappeared in front of my eyes, not bothering to leave through the door. An involuntary shiver racked my body, and chest tight, I sucked in air. My ribs couldn't fill. I stumbled to the balcony doors and threw them open.

Stepping out, I realized it was nearing sunrise, the horizon turning shades of violet and pale yellow. Moving past the patio furniture, I made it to the ivy covered railing, a scattering of white moon flowers amongst the trailing vines beginning to close.

The city lay asleep, except for the sound of birds and a random car noise or two. I could see a jogger on the street, ear buds in, and an elderly woman walking two large dogs.

A black car cruised up to the hotel entrance and I watched a parking attendant, dressed in the standard burgundy and gold suit, climb out. He left the motor running, and I realized it was the same black Porsche I'd seen Mary Lynn in last night.

A woman's musical laughter drifted up from below, but I couldn't see her. Was this Mary Lynn's new girlfriend?

She said something that sounded like a question, although I couldn't make out her actual words. I leaned over the ivy, but the overhang of the hotel's entrance blocked my view. I cocked my head, listening and wondering if my friend was with her. The low murmur of a reply was definitely not Mary Lynn's voice. In fact, it was a male, and a certain one in particular who made my pulse skip.

I checked the sleek automobile again. It definitely looked like the vehicle I'd seen—could there be more than one in town?

Of course, but my gut told me it was the mystery date from last night—or early this morning. When Killion stepped into view, escorting the woman to the driver's side, I felt the balcony floor yawn open. She clung to his arm as though they were a couple, the wide brimmed hat she wore hiding her features.

As if he sensed my eyes on them, Killion glanced up, and being the Peeping Tom I was, I jumped back and ducked behind the ivy. After a moment, pulse in my ears, I peeked between some of the variegated leaves.

The woman faced him, a hand brushing at the lapel of his jacket. Her body language continued to be flirty, and I narrowed my eyes when he smiled down at her, their conversation still too quiet for my ears.

She whipped off the hat and tossed it through the open door, then she kissed his cheek. Jealousy cracked like a whip through me. He accepted her outstretched hand and helped her into the seat.

A mix of shock and other emotions collided when I caught a glimpse of her face. This couldn't be. It was wrong on so many levels. What was Killion doing with *her*?

Since my friend did not appear, I assumed their barhopping had ended early. Had this woman rushed here to hook up with the vampire afterward?

My stomach knotted, my mouth dry. All of Death's warnings about Killion rang in my head.

Marching into the bedroom, I ignored Ghost's bark to play and sent a message to Mary Lynn. My foot tapped and I paced, waiting for a response. When none came, I reached into my bag.

Drawing out the scythe, I smacked it in my open palm. Someone had some 'splainin to do, and I prayed Mary Lynn was still alive.

If not, Jacqueline Vermouth, Grim Reaper 1st Class, along with my mentor, were about to meet a bloody end.

THIRTY-EIGHT

The female vampire, Simone, sat near the exit. She gave me quite a start, because she was so unnaturally still, I nearly blew right past her in my state of determination.

"You may not leave," she said in a sultry voice.

"Holy creeps, Batman!" I exclaimed, grabbing my chest. "Where did you come from?"

Her long, stocking clad legs were crossed, her arms resting on the chair as she eyed the scythe. "Killion insists you are safest here."

Ghost's hackles rose. I tightened my hold on the handle. "And why isn't he playing guard? Oh right, because he's busy screwing a 1st Class grim, who happens to be dating my friend."

She arched an immaculate, narrow brow at my outburst, yet nothing else moved. "It would be wise to return to the bedroom and wait for the master there."

"Like a good little vampire would?"

She kept her emotions controlled like her body, but now I saw a flicker of hatred. It was the same she'd shown at the church. The fingers of her right hand twitched ever so slightly and I figured she was imagining the feel of my neck under them.

"I don't need a watch dog, or a vampire jailer." I pointed to Ghost. "The guard dog position is filled, and no one orders me around."

I reached for the doorknob, and before I could blink, she was there, batting my hand away. "Please return to your quarters."

She was taller than me, especially in her stilettos. Fierce determination burned in her eyes and I felt a well of energy propel me backward. She hated the fact I'd been sleeping in her boss' bedroom. "Am I under house arrest?"

The barest tremor disturbed her ruby red lips and the tips of her fangs flashed. "I am to protect you at all costs. My orders are to keep you inside this suite."

"First of all, I don't need protection." At least not from a vampire who seemed as though she'd be happy to kill me herself. "Secondly, you let Death in. I'd say you failed your assignment with flying colors."

Distressed, she glanced around. "Death?"

"Yeah, you know, the one who can take anyone's life by snapping his fingers? He was just in Killion's bedroom telling me not to trust anyone, including your boss." I raised the scythe, and light from the sconce flashed off the blade. "Move, or it's off with your head."

An internal debate waged behind her eyes. She might have been a big, bad vampire, but my reputation, and the fact she'd seen what I'd done at the church up close and personal, must have given equal weight to Killion's orders.

Either that, or she hoped my enemy *would* kill me. Sure, she'd be at the receiving end of Killion's wrath, but she'd still be alive. She stepped aside.

As I touched the handle, my blood warmed. I felt Killion on the other side. He pulled open the door, blocking my exit. "You're awake."

I lifted the blade. "And you have explaining to do. Again."

He glanced at the weapon with no more care than he would a child's toy. "I'm afraid I require more context."

"Why was Jacqueline here?"

His brow furrowed and he sniffed the air. "Why was Death?"

"Answer me first."

"She required a room for the night. She stays here when she has business in town."

"She doesn't live in Dante's Grove?"

"No. Her work covers multiple jurisdictions, and the population of humans requiring her services keeps her on the road more days than not. Why are you upset by her presence?"

To be honest, it wasn't just her *presence* and what that suggested, but the unabashed flirting she'd done with him. Not only was she supposedly dating Mary Lynn—and I had no idea if they were exclusive, but I was protective of my friend—Killion hadn't seemed overly upset by it. He'd warned me to stay away from her, for my own good. Yet, he'd welcomed her here and left me to go to her? "I saw you downstairs. You seem to be exceptionally friendly with her, after telling me to steer clear. Do you treat all of your visitors so...hands-on?"

He didn't miss a beat, his pupils darkening. Amusement flashed in them. "Why Chloe, are you jealous?"

I chuckled but the sound was forced. "Don't be ridiculous."

The wicked grin was there and gone in a heartbeat. "May I come in?"

It was his place; he had every right to. I didn't move. "Time for one of those hard truths. Are you sleeping with her?"

The grin turned more predatory and made my hackles rise. "Don't be ridiculous," he echoed. "She asked for my advice about an investment. I am not friends with her—and certainly not her lover. Why are you so upset? Has Death planted this idea in your head?"

Relief sneaked through my chest. "This has nothing to do with him." Not really. "Why would she ask your advice about an investment?"

"He owns a financial firm, you idiot," Simone murmured.

Killion shot her a glare over my shoulder. "That will do," he chastised. "Remember your place."

She bit her lower lip and bowed, backing away. "Yes, master."

I waited until she was out of sight, although I assumed she continued listening with her enhanced auditory abilities. "Is that true?"

He nodded. "I have many years of watching businesses and governments rise and fall. I have a sixth sense, you might say, for profitable investments." He swept a hand out in a gesture submitting the opulence all around us as proof.

I so desperately wanted to trust him, but tiny doubts kept sneaking in, like burrs under my skin. Painful, irritating, unwelcome. "She's dating my friend, that's why I'm upset. I don't want to see her hurt. Again. She's had a rough patch with recent relationships."

"Ah." His usual stoic face returned. Detached. "I see."

"I hope you do. If I find out she's cheating on her, I will make her life miserable. It's not nice to toy with humans."

I stepped back and Ghost practically launched herself into his arms as he entered. He caught her and scratched behind one of her ears. "Which friend?"

"Mary Lynn." I headed for the bedroom and my stuff. "The attendant at the morgue, remember? She was going to the pub crawl with Jacqueline and she isn't answering her phone." I was shaking with a combo of fear, dread, and anger. "I have to check on her and make sure she's okay."

He followed, barking out an order to Simone as he walked. "Check on this woman, Mary Lynn...?"

"Haverton," I supplied, stopping to speak over his shoulder. "Don't bother," I called to Simone. The last thing I wanted was her anywhere near one of my friends. "I'll handle it."

In the bedroom, I gathered my things, Death's comment about the church incident being staged, dogging my every move. I snagged my jacket and hefted the bag over my shoulder. I needed to get away from all of them, think things through. The flirting down below threw me off; the fact my friend was dating a grim did as well. Was it possible Killion and Jacqueline were playing me?

As I turned to leave the room, I found the vamp master blocking my path. "I must insist you stay where you are safe."

"Safety is relative, and you need better security to keep Death out." I adjusted my bag's strap. "I won't stay and allow Jacqueline to continue with her plans to hurt people. Get out of my way."

"Grims *are* entitled to a personal life, Chloe, and I doubt she means to harm your friend. Most do find it impossible to keep long-term commitments, especially those with non-magical humans, but being a reaper is lonely work."

If he was in partnership with her, that's exactly what he'd say to throw me off her scent. "You can't hold me here against my will, so either move or I'll become the biggest, loudest, most painful non-magical human you've ever encountered."

A beat of silence passed between us. "Have I not been clear about my position? I would never force you to do anything against your will." He stepped aside, although it seemed to pain him. "But I am truly concerned for your well-being."

"So am I, which is why I'm leaving."

Ghost whimpered and I didn't bother wrestling her from his arms. "Traitor," I murmured to her and walked out. I stopped in the entryway and faced him. The scowl on his face made my guts quiver. "I know you're going to have me followed because you don't believe I can take care of myself." *And if you and Jacqueline are behind the murders, you want to keep tabs on me.* "But let me make *myself* clear. I've been on my own for a while, and I've proven I can handle a whole lot of stuff that others can't. If any of your nest gets in my way, I will—"

He reached for me and I jerked away, not finishing my sentence. What would I do if I ran into Simone or one of the others? I honestly wasn't sure. I needed to find Mary Lynn, question her about Jacqueline.

I needed to talk to Death.

"I'm sorry I've upset you," Killion said, raising his hands in an *I won't touch you* gesture. "Please sit down with me. Let's have breakfast and discuss this."

I wanted to. I hoped this was all a big misunderstanding and I could find the proof that he was innocent, but what did I really know about him outside of what he'd supplied? Was any of that actually true?

"I have to talk to Mary Lynn." *Please let her be okay.* "And I need some time to clear my head."

On the elevator ride down, I wished I'd snagged coffee. Going to The Smoking Bean was out of the question. The rogue was still free, and gunning for me. I wasn't hiding anymore, but I couldn't endanger anyone I cared about, and while I had no doubt Killion would have me followed, I knew it would be foolish to count on a vampire to rush in at any hint of danger and save a friend or colleague for me.

As the elevator sighed to the first floor, my phone rang—a reply from Mary Lynn. Relief swamped me. She assured me she was fine—just hungover and she ended the message with a puking emoji. That was exactly like her, and I was sure the text was genuine.

Me: *Did you have fun on your date?* I asked.

ML: *She's the bomb. I REALLY like her. Oops, gotta go...* Another puking emoji.

I pocketed the phone, considering a return to the penthouse to interrogate Killion in more depth. Had I blown all of this out of proportion? Was I seeing things that weren't there because Death had me paranoid?

My head hurt with all the questions, and although I'd slept well, I still felt mentally and emotionally exhausted. I wanted to rewind to Friday and feel normal again. No serial killers, no grims, no supernatural creatures. Definitely no vampire who made me feel safe one moment and terrified the next.

And if Killion and Jacqueline were really behind all of this, how was I going to stop them? Would Death and SMG help?

I couldn't go home, nor could I go to my aunt and

uncle's. Nita's was definitely out. That only left one place that had very few of the living around.

A cold breeze slid under my jacket when I hit the circular drive outside. Dark clouds moved swiftly across the sky, blotting out the sun. A storm was coming.

I turned left and headed for the morgue.

THIRTY-NINE

Mondays at the morgue can be busy or dead—no pun intended. When I arrived, the place was empty, lights off.

I badged in and didn't bother flicking any lights on as I made my way to the office. According to the roster, the single active case was an elderly lady whose body was waiting for the funeral home to pick her up. She'd been in the hospital and I held my breath while I scanned the info, but she wasn't the woman Talon had tormented. I was relieved.

I checked all the doors and windows to make sure they were locked. Then I made coffee. The grocery store brand tasted like sludge, but it was warm and comforting nonetheless. Once I had a cup, I inhaled deeply, my tight shoulders relaxing slightly and my stomach growling.

Rummaging through the mini-fridge, I remembered about the egg salad sandwich. I discovered a moldy donut, along with a container of Thai takeout I was too squeamish to check for viability. No sandwich, or anything else remotely edible.

I sat at the desk and performed an internet search on Jacqueline Vermouth. Nothing comes that matches what I know about her, although several entries for women of that name or similar pop up in obituaries and marriage licenses.

Mary Lynn's social media pages offer more tangible results. "Score." I see the image of the two of them at a club. It's not a clear shot of Jacqueline, but I copy the picture and do a search on that as well. There are only a few hits, and one leads me to an obit of a woman named Lucinda Balstead who died sixty years ago. The facial similarities suggest she could be a relative.

I stared at Uncle Morty's sign. *We speak for the dead. Respect and honor them. Stick to the facts, and do not suppose you know what their life was like.*

If I could consult him, he'd remind me to stick to the facts. No conjecture, no speculation, just hard truths.

The underground tunnel led to the hospital's basement. No one used the access between the two buildings except during inclement weather. When I entered, a refill in hand, it smelled musty and ancient, a mixture of stagnant water and thick Louisiana clay. Holding a palm to my nose, I went over everything that had happened in the past few days while I walked.

The hospital basement entrance was locked, the door having no modern electronic system and relying on an old-fashioned brass deadbolt. I knocked in hopes a member of the cleaning staff would hear me, and when that didn't raise anyone, I rang the bell that had been installed years ago. It was connected to the front desk and visitor center. I waved up at the tiny security camera posted above the door, and eventually, a janitor let me in.

"Sorry," I said to him. "I know you're busy. I forgot this door isn't electronic."

He was an older fellow with a lazy eye. His good one landed on my cup. "You bring me some coffee and we'll call it even."

The lanyard ID he wore told me his name was Fred. "I'd be happy to, Fred. Cream? Sugar?"

"Black," he replied.

The kitchen was open and busy with the morning rush. Doctors, nurses, and orderlies who knew me said "hi" or nodded as I went through the line. I made sure to get Fred his caffeine payment, along with a cup for myself and a muffin for each of us.

The human resources director, Rachel Simms, was filling her travel mug at the coffee station along the wall. "Chloe, what a surprise to see you here so early. Are you working today?"

I used my fallback excuse. "Paperwork to be filed. Say, you're just the person I need." I pulled out my phone and brought up the photo of Jacqueline. "Do you know this woman?"

"Um, sure, that's the grief counselor from Saint Patrick's parish." Rachel wiped her hand on a napkin and insured her mug was free of spills. "Works with a lot of terminal patients and their families."

"Do you know her name?"

"Ann Jones."

"Not Jacqueline Vermouth?"

She shook her head, adjusting her briefcase strap and picking up her mug. "Pretty name, but no, I'm sure she's Ann Jones. Why?"

Working under the guise of a grief counselor was a pretty good gig for a reaper. "Ever heard of a woman named Lucinda Balstead?"

"Oh sure. She was one of the founders of the hospital's

volunteer service back in the fifties. Her picture is in the gift shop. She had a brush with death and two of our doctors revived her. From that point on, she did lots of things for this place. I have info about her in my files, if you want to read more about her and her contributions here."

Could Jacqueline have been Lucinda back in the day? Volunteering as a way of staying close to the dying? It made sense. She died, the doctors brought her back, and she became a tweener like me. "I'll take you up on that soon. Thanks!"

I took off before she could say anything else. The food and coffees on the tray jiggled as I hustled past the others filing in, a happy buzz of conversations at my back. Unfortunately, Randy appeared.

"Whoa, there." He smiled and reached for my tray, his white lab coat hanging open. "Need help?"

"No, thanks. See you."

"Wait." He caught up to me. I hurried past a painting of downtown Dante's Grove. "Have you seen the latest Marvel film? I thought maybe we could hit the theater this weekend, and…"

I'd never paid attention to the painting, but now saw the stately gothic Beaumont was captured in great detail. A small, brass plaque mentioned that the hotel had made a large donation to the hospital in 1966 for the children's cancer wing. Huh. The master vampire did have a heart of gold.

Randy had stopped speaking. "Chloe?"

My attention shifted to him. I had to nip this in the bud. *Rip the bandage off.* "Sorry, I have so much going on right now. Dating just isn't on my agenda."

"Oh, I meant we could go as friends, that's all."

"No time." I went around him. In another time and

place, he'd be a decent guy to date. Unfortunately, I'd never felt that zing when he was around. "I really have to go."

He called something after me about having a good day, and I waved over my shoulder.

Halfway down the hall, my phone buzzed with a text and I paused to check it. I hoped it was Mary Lynn, but it was Killion. His message nearly made me drop the tray.

Killion: *The rogue has surfaced. Katarina and I are closing in. Would you like to join us?*

I slumped against the nearest wall, praying it was true. If the Undead captured the rogue, I was safe and Killion would be in the clear. Would he be shocked when he discovered Jacqueline under the robes?

'Investment advice,' my robe-covered backside.

I was more and more convinced it was her. Placing the phone on the tray, I debated how to respond. I pushed off the wall and continued to the basement. Should I meet with him and Katarina? If it was Jacqueline, she was highly dangerous, and even if it wasn't? The rogue had gone to great lengths to outsmart all of us. What would he or she do when trapped?

I worried my bottom lip, suddenly and annoyingly concerned for Killion's safety. Laughable, that, but I couldn't help it.

Holding the tray with one arm, I clumsily replied.
Me: *Be careful.*

I added that I believed our culprit was Jacqueline, then deleted it. I had no proof, and regardless of what he'd claimed, she exuded power, confidence, beauty—the same as him. He might not be her friend—or lover—but anything I said against her at this point would probably be disregarded following my earlier accusations.

Tough. I finished the message anyway.

Me: *You won't believe me, but the rogue is Jacqueline. I don't know what she was after this morning, but it wasn't investment advice.*

My thumb hovered over the Send button. What did I have to lose? I'd already put a wall between us, and I had to warn him. I let the message fly.

I needed to protect Mary Lynn, too, but that would be an even more difficult conversation, and one I wanted to have in person. If Killion caught Jacqueline today, maybe I wouldn't need to.

"Special delivery for Fred," I called when I entered the janitorial area. One-handing the tray again, I shoved the phone in my jacket. All was quiet, except for a rattling, gasping sound. I wondered if there was a generator or furnace nearby. "Fred?"

I peeked around the corner and pulled up short. He lay on the floor near the tunnel's door, grabbing at his chest. His mouth opened and closed like a fish sucking at air.

I dropped the tray and rushed to his side. "Fred, stay with me." I glanced around and yelled, "Help!"

There was nobody there, except the two of us. My fingers shook as I hit the speed dial button for the main number. When the operator answered, I told her what was happening and where we were. "He's having a heart attack. I need a doctor now!"

She told me to stay on the line and I heard her call to someone nearby. A second later she was back. "They're on their way," she told me.

Dropping the phone, I whipped off my jacket and balled it up under Fred's head. "Doctors are coming. Look at me, Fred. You're going to be okay."

His eyes rolled up, and my blood ran cold. A figure in

black robes and a face mask stepped from the shadows, fingers extended toward him.

"Hello, Chloe." The grim wore a mask and the voice was electronically synthesized. A black gloved hand motioned toward the open door. "If you want to save him, get in the tunnel."

FORTY

Fred was fading fast, his gasps fewer and farther between. "I want your promise you'll let him live." Moving to the door, I put a hand on the knob. "Swear it, Jacqueline."

"Look at you. Not even three full days on the job and you guessed it was me. Overachiever."

"Fred is innocent. Let him go."

"I hardly think you're in a position to negotiate."

I wasn't. "I'm all yours. You've got what you want."

With a dramatic sigh, she waved a hand over him and he took a sharp, deep breath. "There. Now move."

I glanced down at the poor man. "You'll be okay." The sound of an approaching team came from the hallway. I wanted to stay, and wished they could help me along with Fred, but Jacqueline might kill a few—or all—of them if I didn't do what she wanted.

Taking on the rogue reaper alone in the tunnel was the worst idea ever, but what choice did I have? *If only I had my scythe or robes...*

I bolted through the door at the same time three medical personnel entered the unit. I heard a guy call my name, but I ran. I had one chance to survive—get to my bag in the morgue.

My feet pounded on the damp stone floor, the clang of the door slamming behind me like a nail hammering into my coffin. "Death," I called. "If you can hear me, now would be a good time to help a grim out."

He didn't show, but Jacqueline had definitely joined me. "Stop." That electronic voice was super annoying, especially when the acoustics of the tunnel made it echo. "You can't escape."

Escape...escape...escape... The word rebounded around me.

Escaping wasn't the plan, but I picked up my pace. There had to be a reason she hadn't tried to kill me face-to-face, and I was betting it had to do with my scythe, and/or Ghost being present. I wasn't a 'wannabe' grim—I was the real deal. The robes had chosen me. And while I wasn't a magical creature, I seemed to have a knack for being a reaper.

The passage swerved as I neared the morgue. The terrible lighting kept me from seeing a puddle of water on the floor and when my foot made contact, I slid.

My ankle twisted and I fell, searing pain shooting up my calf. The impact of hitting the hard stone floor knocked the breath from my lungs and I lay dazed for several seconds. My gaze landed on the water pooled on the floor, and I realized it was crimson. The metallic tang in the air told me it was blood.

There wasn't only a puddle of it, either. My eyes tracked the thin stream to a shadowed corner.

"Chloooo...eeee," Mary Lynn was propped between the

two walls, the blood coming from her. Her voice was child-like, weary. "Help me."

I scrambled to my feet, my ankle barking in pain. Hobbled, I pitched toward her. My palm skidded on the stone floor and tears beaded in my eyes from the searing heat going up and down my calf. I crawled the last foot to reach her. "What happened?"

"You have to do what she says," her voice, breathless, hitched. "Or she'll...kill me."

Even this close, I couldn't tell where the wound was located. I'd left my jacket with Fred. Blood covered her arms and hands and I jerked my shirt off. "Where are you hurt? We need to stop the bleeding."

I shivered, the cold air biting my skin. She stared at my tattoo, over the cup of my bra, but shoved the balled garment away. "Just do what she says. *Please.*" The last word was a whisper.

"You can't hide from me, Chloe." Jacqueline's voice buzzed, her footsteps now close.

Kill.

The door was two feet away. "I need my bag," I told Mary Lynn. "I'll be right back, I promise."

As I began to crawl, she gripped my arm. "Don't leave me," she whispered desperately. "I'm scared."

The sound of my friend begging nearly tore me apart. I hated all of them—Jacqueline, SMG, Death, even Killion. They were all playing games with people's lives. "I will protect you," I told her, removing her fingers from my arm. The blade sang its death song in my head. "Don't give up."

As fast as I could, I dragged myself to the door. Using it for leverage, I grasped the levered knob and heaved myself to standing.

The lever didn't give. Someone had locked it from the inside.

"No, no, no." I beat at the old wood and yanked again.

I threw my weight against it and ended up yelping from the fresh twinge that ripped up my leg. I lost my balance and dropped, curses falling from my mouth. I gritted my teeth against the scream in my throat and the tears in my eyes.

Jacqueline rounded the corner, sure of herself and the outcome of this meeting. She knew I couldn't get inside for my bag. She'd thwarted my escape and blocked my way.

Stopping a few feet from me, she still wore the mask. I could sense the comic relief on her face when she took in my defeat and chuckled. "You're a fighter. I admire that." She closed in and the hair on the back of my neck became electrified. "We could be so powerful if we worked together."

Kill.

My brain cells wanted to short circuit as I processed her statement. "Are you insane?" Door at my back, I sent out another mental SOS to Death, or anyone else who could help for that matter. "Reaping my soul is murder. The Soul Management Group will not stand for it. Even if I fail to stop you, there will be others. Killion will –"

She cut me off. "Killion craves power as much as I do, and I can give it to him. He tasted you that night, just like I did." A gloved finger stroked my cheek. "When Gustafson killed you, the rush was..." Behind the mask, her lids fluttered with a look of nirvana. "Your essence is not one I've ever tasted. It's intoxicating." Her gaze met mine once more. "I need more of it. More of *you.*"

"Yield to her," Mary Lynn crawled to my side. She

stroked my arm. "She's going to create a whole new world for us."

I shifted sideways, my balance unsteady, unsure of what exactly was going on. I felt a new depth to how far my stomach could sink. "What did you do to her?" Mary Lynn no longer seemed scared or injured, her eyes glittering in the low light. "You can manipulate humans, can't you?"

Mary Lynn grinned. "You're so beautiful, Chloe. So smart. I'm not under any kind of enchantment. I *believe*."

"Believe what? That Jacqueline is *not* a psychotic maniac?"

"You felt the power," the manic whispered in my ear, pinning me against the wall. She tugged gently on my braid. The edge of the door frame pressed into my spine, and she brought her other hand to my chest, fingers splayed. Molten heat flooded my rib cage. "This power. Doesn't it feel good?"

The sensation I'd associated previously with anger caught, a white-hot inferno raging through me. I sucked in a ragged breath, gasping for cool air to quench my burning lungs and blazing organs. I half-expected my hair to self-combust. "Stop...it," I ground out.

"Give in to it," she murmured seductively. Her mask was rough on my cheek. "Come on, Chloe. Ride it with me."

Mary Lynn threaded her arm through mine, licking her lips.

I closed my eyes, sick with the thought of her betraying me. I wanted to lash out, punch something, yell at the top of my lungs, but my limbs were paralyzed. "I will *never* yield."

My tattoo lit. A fresh flush of energy spread through me, the pain instantly gone and my mind clear. The buzzing noise was back in my ears and my heart thumped a too-quick beat. I was flying, weightless and giddy.

Not even three shots of espresso on an empty stomach felt this good. I fought not to succumb to it, but the waves of bliss were tantalizing. *No pain. No worry. No fear.*

Only power.

"We hold control over life and death." Jacqueline's voice was now that of an angel, light and loving. "Taste the euphoria of the gods. This is what it feels like to create and destroy by your will."

My vision blanked out and I was floating on a wind current. There was no past or future, only right here, right now. I was above all of the strife and the grief. I could do anything. Go anywhere.

"*Chloe.*" The sound of my mother's voice interrupted my bliss. "She's using you! Fight it. Remember who you are."

The dream, the bliss turned sour. My lids flew open. "Mom?

"That's sweet." Jacqueline tilted her head. Her voice was her own again and she'd removed the mask. "I'm not really the mother type, but sure, kid. Whatever gets you onboard."

Rage ripped through me. With strength I didn't know I had, I knocked her hand from my chest. The spell broke. The paralyzing coma evaporated. The pain in my leg came back with a fury, but I savored it. "You couldn't even be my dog."

I shoved her away with all my might. She flew backward. Mary Lynn squealed and reached for her, and the two of them ended up on the ground.

"Mom? Are you here?" My gaze scanned the tunnel, all

the nooks and crannies hidden in the shadows. I staggered to my feet, desperate to find her.

My mother did not appear. What did, however, was the only tool I had.

The shades. They zoomed around the corner and hovered, circling all three of us. Jacqueline shoved Mary Lynn off and jumped to her feet. The howling banshee cries rang out, echoing through the passageway, but it didn't bother me this time. I welcomed it, the frequency vibrating in my very bones. I could see it shimmering in the air around me, just like I'd seen the magic of the church. It shielded me from her. Things began to click into place and I narrowed my eyes at her. "Where's your scythe?"

She stood tall, ignoring the screeching of the souls she'd bound to her, but I could read uncertainty now in her eyes. It was only a flicker, there and gone in an instant, but I'd caused a crack in her armor, and the shades were going to help me bust it wide open.

"I don't need it to take your soul." She flung out a hand, but the magic she used had no effect this time. The cry of the souls protected me. My mother, too, her encouragement defeating the addictive taste of Jacqueline's power.

"Magic," I seethed. "You're not some powerful reaper like you've convinced everyone you are. You're a magician, illusion-ing all of us. You need the energy of the souls to feed that magic, and that's why you've gone rogue. Not to build an army of grims, but rather, a constant supply of power to fuel your spells."

The shades' cries escalated and Mary Lynn covered her ears and staggered toward the wall. "Make it stop!"

"Don't be ridiculous," Jacqueline yelled at me. "I'm a master grim. You'll never be as powerful as I am, but you can be my channel for the power. Amp me up. A powerful reaper in your own right. I'll give you everything you want, everything you deserve."

I didn't know that much about magic, illusions, or even power, but I sure wasn't interested in what she was offering. "What I want right now is for you to die."

She bared her teeth, rage turning her beautiful features ugly. Before I could move, she attacked.

FORTY-ONE

The blow from her fist snapped my head back, the stones behind me unforgiving when my skull struck with a sickening thud. Stars danced across my vision and my legs wobbled.

"You don't think I'm a grim?" She screeched, nearly drowning out the shades. "You stupid, stupid girl."

With one hand, she grabbed Mary Lynn by the hair, and quicker than I could blink, I heard the zing of a blade. Her scythe emerged from under her robes and Mary Lynn screamed.

I blinked away the dizziness. "You can't kill her." I threw out a hand in a stop gesture. "Her contract's not up. It's not her time!"

The shades surged forward. Jacqueline held my friend in a chokehold, twirling the weapon in her other hand. "I am the most powerful grim on earth, and I decide when it's her time to die." The blade rose.

Fear exploded inside me, and I yelled, diving at them. As my body slammed into theirs, the three of us went down. The blade sliced through my arm. Blood splattered.

Jacqueline was strong, but with the weight of Mary Lynn and myself on top of her, she couldn't escape. Her scythe waved through the air, the needle-sharp end nearly jabbing my eye. As she swung again awkwardly, I rolled, reaching for her wrist.

The cold edge of the blade slid through my palm, slicing it open. Through the pain, I closed my fingers around it and hung on.

It hummed and tingled against my wound, seeming to suck at my blood. My heart did a funny tap dance and my veins sang with true power. A new and different form of warmth poured through me, a familiar and welcome sensation.

Killion was near.

I shoved Mary Lynn off Jacqueline. "Run!"

The grim jerked the handle of her weapon, and the scythe sunk deeper into my palm. It would surely cut my hand in half if I didn't let go.

The shades writhed and wailed. Jacqueline tried to rock me off her. Grabbing her wrist with my free hand, I slammed hers on the ground. The scythe was covered in my blood, the pain distant, my awareness starting to float away. *So...much...blood...*

Blinking, I forced myself to focus. I thought of Nita, of Ghost. I thought of my aunt and uncle. Of Killion. A fresh surge of adrenaline hit and I slammed Jacqueline's hand down over and over again. Once, twice, three times, I beat her knuckles into the blood-wet floor. My head swam, the spots in my peripheral vision back and growing larger. I didn't need to see, *just stay conscious.*

The door handle jiggled. "Chloe?" Killion's voice sounded far away, but I was nearly giddy to hear it. "Are you in there?"

"Help," I squeaked, leveraging my weight to slam my knee into Jacqueline's rib cage.

The door burst open, wood shattering. "Here!" He tossed the robes at me.

Fluttering down over me like a hundred black feathers, I felt the fabric wrap itself around my body. A new rush of that strange adrenaline they offered hit my system and I seized up for a breath and let it.

At the same time, the Grim 1st Class finally released her grip on the scythe. "No," she wheezed. "You can't do this!"

The cutting steel warmed in my blood-soaked palm. Instead of releasing it, I gripped it harder, feeling a tickle, rather than pain, now.

Killion strode forward, his monster on display, and reached for Jacqueline. "You," he growled and the hair on the back of my neck stood up. "I will kill you."

"Help me, Killion," she begged. "It's her. She's the one!"

I smacked her across the face with my free hand. Her robes quivered. So did her scythe.

Bliss—I felt it again, my blood drawing her magic out. Drawing her grimness to me.

I could take it. Take all of her beauty, her power, her...life.

Killion reached for her throat and seethed. "Don't you dare try to blame Chloe."

I smacked his hands away. "Mine."

"No, please! She wants to kill me! Killion, don't let her—"

Her words were choked off as the shades, acting as one, dove into her open mouth. The column of smoky spectrals made her eyes bug out and she choked and coughed.

Killion touched my shoulder. "Don't kill her, Chloe. Bring her to justice."

Kill, the scythe taunted. *She is not worthy.*

I wanted to. If anyone deserved it, it was her. A part of me wanted to wring every bit of her lifeforce from her, ride the high her soul would give me if I did.

She struggled and I slammed my hand down on her chest. Her essence teased me like the drug it was. All I had to do was send the blade at her throat...

Her struggling ceased and she froze, staring at me. *Do it*, her eyes seemed to say.

Or maybe that was my imagination, giving me permission to become a monster just like she was.

Ghost barked and jumped on her chest, knocking my hand away. She looked me in the eye and wagged her tail. She was ready to take Jaqueline's soul to the other side. *If that's what I wanted.*

Something about the three-pound puppy reminded me of life. Of laughing and love. I wasn't after power or prestige. I didn't care about magic, or living forever. I saved people and animals. *I do not kill them.*

All the fight went out of me, and I slid to the side, still gripping the blade.

The floor rose up to meet me, but my nose suddenly stopped about an inch from the stones. Strong hands lifted me.

"You can release the scythe, now," Killion said gently. He cradled me against his chest.

Ghost morphed into her psychopomp self, pinning Jacqueline to the floor. The woman didn't fight anymore because of it. Or perhaps the shades had her locked up tight.

The master carried me to the open door, Simone and

Katarina, rushed in, descending on Jacqueline and assisting Mary Lynn.

My fingers went numb. The blade dropped, clanging on the floor. "I found the rogue," I muttered.

"You sure did."

"How did you know I was here?"

"I always know where you are. My blood is in your veins."

"Gross," I whispered, barely able to keep my eyes propped open.

Killion chuckled as he carried me out, the sound that rumbled in his chest a purr to my ears. "You are safe now."

Safe. *Yes.* I closed my eyes and let exhaustion take me.

FORTY-TWO

I woke in the bedroom at the hotel and not in the hospital. The blinds were drawn and it took me a full minute to gain my bearings. Even when Ghost landed on my chest, and Killion leaned over the bed to smile at me, I wondered if it was only a dream.

"How do you feel?" he asked.

My mouth was dry as cotton, my brain riding a fuzzy, drug-induced wave. Ghost showered me with kisses, making happy whining noises. I couldn't feel much of my body, tucked under the satin sheets and heavy comforter. "Hungry, I think," I muttered, but my lips weren't cooperating and "hungry" came out sounding like "horny."

The lamp on the bedside table came on, and I saw Killion's frown. He looked slightly surprised. "Well, that's...unusual."

I lifted my heavy hand, noticed the cloth wrapping my palm, and managed to scrub my face. Ghost sniffed at the bandage. "Hun-gry," I tried again. This time, it came out more accurate.

His expression turned to one of relief. "Ah, good. That means you're nearly healed."

He tugged the chair he'd been occupying closer to the bed, shifting an IV pole out of the way. "You gave me, *us*, quite a scare."

Elbowing myself up, I became frustrated when the line in my arm tangled around the puppy when she hopped aside. "Is Mary Lynn okay?"

He untangled the dog and rearranged the pillows to prop me up. Then he poured me a glass of water from the pitcher on the nightstand. "She is fine. Jacqueline put her under a compulsion, but it's broken now. She has no memory of what happened. Her injury was faked, and while she's recovering from a magic-induced hangover, she believes it stems from too much alcohol."

I drank deeply. The water was the best thing I'd tasted in a long time. "And Fred?"

"Fully recovered and crediting you with saving his life."

Ghost found a toy and snuggled down to chew on it. "What did he say about Jacqueline?"

"He called her what she was—a grim reaper—and he does believe it was his time to go. The doctors, along with his family and friends, have chalked it up to the trauma of the heart attack."

So that part was real, and not an illusion. I finished off the drink. "Is she dead? Jacqueline?"

Killion took the empty glass and offered more, but I waved it off. "Alive, but in a secure containment unit at SMG. She will be dealt with. She is the one responsible for the death of the Jensens, along with nine others, both supernatural and non. I feel a great weight that I did not stop her sooner."

"You and me, both." Two sets of robes hung, clean and

neatly pressed, on the doors of the armoire on the other side of the room. One had a missing chunk from the lower left hem. "Why are those here?"

"Her robes left her and secured themselves to you as I carried you from the morgue. You had passed out at that point. I believe they were comforting you."

I rubbed my forehead with my good hand. My hair was loose and a few strands tangled in my trappings. "No, absolutely not. I can't handle the set I have. I'm not taking hers, too. How does that even work? I can't be two grims at once."

Killion smiled. "It is a detail that will have to be worked out, but you are an enigma, as I have mentioned. The robes seem to be grateful for your service and want to work with you."

My stomach growled. I held out my arm. "Can we get rid of this?"

He tenderly took my wrist, undoing the tape holding the line to my skin. Removing the tubing, he hung it on the pole, then carefully slid the needle out of my vein. A drop of blood emerged and his gaze rose to mine, his eyes going melty and seductive.

My pulse skipped, but I didn't draw away. I simply held his gaze and swallowed.

"You lost a lot of blood and required a transfusion, but I assure you, it's not from me."

My vision seemed to narrow until he was the only thing I saw. "Jacqueline said my spirit's essence was unlike any she'd ever tasted when Gustafson killed me. Am I some kind of...freak?"

The side of his mouth quirked. The warmth of his touch soothed me. "I'm not sure how to classify you, but I do believe you're more than human."

He reached in the drawer and brought out an alcohol

wipe and bandage. In a second, the blood was gone. "Ready for sustenance?" He held out a hand in invitation.

Boy, was I. If nothing else, this grim gig made me ravenous. I allowed him to help me stand and together, we ventured to the buffet waiting for us in the dining room.

I WAS ten minutes late to the library on campus. Nita was biting a nail when I arrived and looked relieved to see me. "There you are. I was about to text you."

I would've been even later if it hadn't been for Killion's driver. "Sorry, I lost track of time." I dropped my messenger bag on to the table between us.

She studied me with a knowing perusal. "There's definitely something different about you. You're practically glowing."

I ignored her sly grin, and unpacked my anatomy book. The heavy edition thudded on the scarred wood of the table. I felt strong and was grateful to be alive. Whether due to my new job, or perhaps a vampire's blood, I didn't know, and right now, I didn't care. "What do you want to start with?"

"Tell me he's good in bed."

"Nita!"

"What?" She feigned mock innocence. "Hey, I need to live vicariously through you, Morticia. The only way I'm going to get any is if I take back Joey Mulhern."

I flipped open the book to a sticky noted page. "I only met Killion Friday night. I don't even know him yet." That felt like tart grapes on my tongue. I knew him far better than I cared to admit.

"He's rich, gorgeous, and seems to care for you. What else do you need to know?"

Everything. There was still so much I wanted to learn about him. "I thought you wanted to study."

She gave an exasperated huff and opened her laptop. "Give him my number, will you?" The grin returned. "I mean, if you're truly not interested in him…?"

I rolled my eyes. "You have no self-respect."

Darcy stumbled by, stopped, and rushed back to us. "Are you going to the Alpha Epsilon Halloween gig Friday night? It's a costume party." She singsonged the last few words, as if costumes made it more inviting. Maybe they did.

"Of course," Nita replied. "Wouldn't miss it."

Darcy made a finger gun and pulled the imaginary trigger. "I'm going with Larson and we're dressing as Bonnie and Clyde!"

She whisked herself off and Nita looked at me expectantly. "We should go."

I mimicked Darcy and put the imaginary gun to my temple. "Nope."

"Come on, Chloe. Let's be normal college girls this weekend. No studying—just partying."

"I have Saturday morning shift at The Bean."

"So what? You don't sleep anyway."

I'd slept ten hours out of the last sixteen. It was amazing how much better I felt.

Tapping my pen on the textbook, I actually considered it. I seemed to have enhanced strength, the wherewithal to stand my ground, and amazing healing abilities. I wondered how much alcohol I'd need to consume to feel drunk and how long it would take my body to process it. Purely scientific reasons, of course, to test a theory. "Tell you what, you pass this test and I'll go. You fail? We stay in and watch creepy Halloween movies."

"Either way, do you think Pete would be my date?"

"As in, Rogan? Are you seriously going to ask a cop to a frat kegger?"

"You're taking your billionaire boyfriend."

"Am not," I protested. The very thought made me laugh. Killion would probably choke if I suggested it. "Trust me, he has far better things to do than watch a bunch of kids get drunk. But if you want to invite Pete, I say go for it."

"Nah, you're right. That might be awkward for him." She dropped her chin into her palm, her elbow resting on her textbook. "I need to come up with something, though. Something...mature."

I grabbed my notebook. "We'll make a list and you can think about it. See what fits and try it when he comes by The Bean next week."

Her grin made me smile, too. She held out her fist. "Deal."

I bumped it. "Deal."

FORTY-THREE

Friday evening, I was in front of the mirror sticking a pair of my mother's hoop earrings in my ears when Death showed up.

"A gypsy?" He leaned on the doorframe of the bathroom, looking over my long, colorful skirt and bustier top. My playlist was up loud and he spoke over it. "Thought you'd go as a grim."

"Shh!" I held a finger to my lips, then pointed downstairs. "Vera will hear you."

Ghost ran to greet him, and he whirled a finger, dropping that nearly invisible curtain around us to silence our conversation. It glowed a soft lavender and I instantly relaxed a smidge.

"Grim? Get it?" He laughed at his own wit and scooped up the dog.

In the mirror, I watched her shower him with kisses. We really needed to talk about her unhealthy love for him. "I knew it was too good to last," I muttered, slipping in the other earring and reducing the volume of my music. Both Nita and I passed the test with flying colors, and even

Professor O'Leary commented on my 97% grade. Being true to my word, I had to pony up and go to the costume party. "It was such a lovely, normal, three days without you. I was hoping you were going to leave me alone for a while."

Setting Ghost down, he play-punched my shoulder. "Killion and I stayed out of your hair so you could regroup after what happened. I'm not here to keep you from your party, only to let you know that Smudgy and I are happy with your work. You're looking at a nice bonus that should hit your account about....now." He pointed at my cell and a ping echoed from it with a notification from my bank. I opened the app, and sure enough, there'd been a deposit. At the number of zeroes it contained, I nearly dropped the phone.

"Your student loans are gone, too," he continued. "Your schooling from here on out is paid for by a generous benefactor, and your probationary period is over, effective immediately. Killion told me you are reluctant to quit your jobs, but it's necessary. You can stay in school to prepare for your future, but Grim 281 1st Class, you need to be available twenty-four/seven for Smudgy."

A bonus *and* a promotion. Nothing better than a gold star. Two, in this case.

Bribery and manipulation, however, aren't my jam. Like the lies I'd told Nita, this tasted like sour grapes. "I'm under contract for a year, then I'm free, but for now I'm doing this on my terms. I'm keeping my jobs and staying in school. I also want your word that my family and friends will be protected from any fallout associated with my job."

While Mary Lynn showed no signs of memory or distress over what had happened, I couldn't take the chance another innocent could end up hurt or dead because of me.

He smirked, setting the dog down. "Negotiating with Death, again?"

"This isn't a negotiation." I was beginning to believe that I might be as unique as Killion claimed. SMG wanted me for a reason. Death did, too. "Those are my terms. And by the way, speaking of our last contract between us, Vera gets a full ten years."

His eyes bore into mine, the predator trying to back down the prey. I straightened and stayed strong.

The moment passed as quickly as it came. "Fine, but you agree to keep going to therapy."

My brows hit my hairline. "And tell Dr. Maxwell what? I have a new outlook on death and dying?"

"You're carrying a lot here." He touched the spot above my heart. My tattoo warmed. The sensation flooded through my ribcage. "Stuff you haven't processed yet, much less let go of."

"Why did I only hear my mom? Is my dad okay?"

"He's fine. She is, too. Their contracts were up, that's all. It wasn't your fault." Before I asked how he knew I secretly wondered if it was, he glanced at Ghost, who rolled over and over on the carpet, and rubbed her snout into it, wiggling her backside in joyful abandon. I kind of wanted to join her. "Vera has her ten years, Grave Girl. I'll see what I can do about the rest."

Breathing deep, I girded myself for an argument and held out a hand, palm up. "I want it in writing, sealed with your blood."

He chuckled. "Killion said you grew a pair."

Killion—he haunted my dreams, but the bare-bones texts he'd sent asking how I was had been short and, well, just like him, to be honest. Detached, unemotional. Yet, I knew he'd had members of his nest keeping an eye on me. "You two getting along now?"

He took my hand, cupping it in his. It was electrifying, sending goosebumps over my skin. I felt a sharp prick in my palm and the warm sensation of blood. He drew me closer to him, holding our combined hands to his chest as the blood pact was initiated. "I'm keeping you together for investigative work."

My body trembled as I felt the power in his blood mix with mine. "He doesn't need me," I choked out.

"I do." His eyes were mesmerizing, his voice soft, all traces of accent gone. "I need you to keep an eye on him. Keep him in line. You're a reaper, first and foremost, and you'll need to handle the shades, but I still don't trust him. Never will. You'll be my eyes and ears."

Was it like a compulsion, or was it something more human that made me want to do anything he asked at that moment? "You could make millions with that come-hither-and-bend-to-my-will thing."

His smile was feral and conceit shone in his eyes. "I don't need money, and I have plenty of groupies happy to do my bidding."

The image that conjured made my face screw up. "TMI, dude." I forced myself to break eye contact, tugging at his grip. "The shades Jacqueline created—what happened to them?"

He released me, the slit in my palm instantly healing. "They're no longer bound by her spell, and when we took her to SMG, they vamoosed. You can start working on them Monday." He gave a wink and headed for the exit that led to the outside stairs. "Have fun at the party."

"What if I don't want to be Killion's partner?" I called. The thought of him made my heart do somersaults in my chest. We made a good team and a part of me definitely *did* want to work with him, but I feared what might happen between us. My heart couldn't handle it.

"Too bad."

"But...but... He's a vampire!" *And his nest hates me.* "We are from very different worlds. I feel like a..."—*rookie.* I couldn't say it out loud. "There has to be someone else more experienced you can match him up with. He won't even tell me his real name."

"He's always refused to work with a partner. You're the first he's agreed to. Take it as a compliment." At the doorjamb, he turned to give me that trademark smirk. "Guess you'll have to *grim* and *bare* it." He winked. "See what I did there? You're the grim, he's got fangs." He showed me his incisors and made biting motions.

When I didn't laugh, he rolled his eyes and disappeared into the night, the door swinging closed behind him. "Reapers," I heard him say, "always so dead serious."

Ghost barked and rushed to me. I scooped her up and held her close, relieved he was gone for now. A little grateful Killion and I were still a couple. *Not a couple— partners.* "You're going to have to help me keep these males in line," I told her.

My phone buzzed with a text.

Killion: *I now have a question for you.*

This should be interesting. Me: *Shoot.*

Killion: *There are witches, wizards, werewolves, trolls, unicorns, and many other creatures in Harry Potter, but no vampires?*

My pulse danced. Me: *You watched the movies?*

Killion: *I have read the books and watched the movies. The books are better.*

I laughed. Me: *Can we discuss it in more depth tonight after the party?*

Killion: *I would welcome that.*

So would I. Footsteps echoed on the interior stairs and Nita burst in. "Let's go. Killion's waiting for us."

"What? You're kidding!"

She'd dressed as a gypsy, too, so we could be twins. Her wicked grin told me she'd invited him. "I know, right? It's like he can read your mind or something. But we should totally take advantage of it. That limo? To die for." She hip-bumped me. "We will arrive in style."

My cheeks heated with embarrassment. Hopefully, he didn't plan to stay. No way was I getting drunk if he did. That's all I needed— for him to have ammunition to tease me about down the road.

Secretly, I was happy I was going to see him, though. I'd make short work of the costume party and spend time with him afterward. Maybe he'd feed me again.

Maybe I'd coerce his real name from him.

"You're glowing," Nita teased with a wink. "Goodbye, Morticia Addams, hello Chloe Frost, slayer of hearts every-where. Ready?"

I kissed Ghost's head, then gave her a treat and put her on the bed. "Yes," I said, a new surge of confidence sweeping through me. Tonight, I was going to enjoy being young and no longer sleep deprived. Monday, it was back to work as a grim. I thought about Killion downstairs in the limo and I couldn't keep the goofy smile off my face. "I'm ready."

Paranormal Contemporary Romance

Witches Anonymous Step 1

Jingle Hells, WA Step 2

Wicked Souls, WA Step 3

Dark Moon Lilith, Witches Anonymous Step 4

Dancing With the Devil, Witches Anonymous Step 5

Devil's Due, Witches Anonymous Step 6

Dirty Deeds, Witches Anonymous Step 7

Wicked Wedding, Witches Anonymous Step 8

Urban Fantasy

Revenge Is Sweet, Kali Sweet Urban Fantasy Series, Book 1

Sweet Chaos, Kali Sweet Urban Fantasy Series, Book 2

Sweet Soldier, Kali Sweet Urban Fantasy Series, Book 3

Sweet Curse, Kali Sweet Urban Fantasy Series, Book 4

Paranormal Romantic Suspense

Soul Survivor, Moon Water Series, Book 1

Soul Protector, Moon Water Series, Book 2

Cozy Mysteries (writing as Nyx Halliwell)

Sister Witches Of Raven Falls Mystery Series

Of Potions and Portents

Of Curses and Charms

Of Stars and Spells

Of Spirits and Superstition

Confessions of a Closet Medium Cozy Mystery Series

Pumpkins & Poltergeists

Magic & Mistletoe

Hearts & Haunts

Vows & Vengeance

Cupcakes & Corpses

Once Upon a Witch Cozy Mystery Series

If the Cursed Shoe Fits (Cinder)

Beastly Book of Spells (Belle)

Poisoned Apple Potion (Snow) - only available in the Black Cat Crossing box set which is FREE when you sign up for the Whiskered Mysteries newsletter!

Red Hot Wolfie (Ruby)

Hexed Hair Day (Rapunzel)

Don't want to miss a single release? Click here and get a FREE story (or two… :))

SEALs of Shadow Force Series

Fatal Truth

Fatal Honor

Fatal Courage

Fatal Love

Fatal Vision

Fatal Thrill

Risk

SEALS of Shadow Force Series: Spy Division

Man Hunt

Man Killer

Man Down

The SCVC Taskforce Series

Deadly Pursuit

Deadly Deception

Deadly Force

Deadly Intent

Deadly Affair, A SCVC Taskforce novella

Deadly Attraction

Deadly Secrets

Deadly Holiday, A SCVC Taskforce novella

Deadly Target

Deadly Rescue

Deadly Bounty

Deadly Betrayal

Deadly Threat

The Super Agent Series

Operation Sheba

Operation Paris

Operation Proof of Life

Operation Lost Princess

Operation Ambush

Operation Christmas Contraband

Operation Sleeping With the Enemy

The Justice Team Series (with Adrienne Giordano)

Stealing Justice

Cheating Justice

Holiday Justice

Exposing Justice

Undercover Justice

Protecting Justice

Missing Justice

Defending Justice

SCHOCK SISTERS MYSTERY SERIES w/Adrienne Giordano

1st Shock

2nd Strike

3rd Tango

The Secret Ingredient Culinary Mystery Series

The Secret Ingredient, A Culinary Romantic Mystery with Bonus Recipes

The Secret Life of Cranberry Sauce, A Secret Ingredient Holiday Novella

MEET MISTY

USA TODAY Bestselling Author Misty Evans has published over seventy-five novels and writes romantic suspense, urban fantasy, and paranormal romance. Under her pen name, Nyx Halliwell, she also writes cozy mysteries.

When not reading or writing, she embraces her inner gypsy and loves music, movies, and hanging out with her husband, twin sons, and three spoiled puppies. She's a crafter at heart and has far too many projects to finish.

Don't want to miss a single adventure? Visit www.mistyevansbooks.com to find out ALL the news!

Check out her humorous pen name Nyx Halliwell for magical mysteries https://www.nyxhalliwell.com .

LETTER FROM MISTY

Hello Beautiful Reader!

Thank you for reading this story! It is an honor and a privilege to write stories for you.

I hope you enjoyed this book, and I'd like to ask a favor – would you mind leaving a review at your favorite retailer? I'd really appreciate it, and reviews help other readers find books they will love too.

If you'd like to learn about my other books, sales, and special promotions, please sign up for my newsletter at www.readmistyevans.com.

Grab special edition box sets and get new releases before they come out at retailers by visiting my direct buy website www.mistyevansbooks.com. I have sales and offer NEW RELEASES early and at a discount!! Check it out.

Last but not least, if you enjoy clean, cozy mysteries, visit my pen name www.nyxhalliwell.com to see those books!

Thank you and happy reading!
Misty